"WHAT ARE YOU DOING?" MAGGIE'S VOICE QUIVERED.

"Sometimes," Hank said quietly, "it's necessary to illustrate a point." Without another word, he swept Maggie into his arms and kissed her with fierce intensity.

Maggie pushed him away. "You're crazy. This whole thing is crazy. I'm just biding my time here. Don't you realize that? As soon as I can, I'll be gone. Why complicate matters?"

"They're already complicated, Maggie. Love does that to people."

"Love? Come on, Hank. We hardly know each other."

"Oh, I wouldn't say that. I know a lot about you. I know that you have a terrific laugh, a dramatic temper, a wealth of tender feelings, passion—and someday you're going to love me. That's all I need to know."

CANDLELIGHT ECSTASY ROMANCES®

THE BITTER
WITH
THE SWEET

Alison Tyler

A CANDLELIGHT ECSTASY ROMANCE®

Published by
Dell Publishing Co., Inc.
1 Dag Hammarskjold Plaza
New York, New York 10017

Dell ® TM 681510, Dell Publishing Co., Inc.

Candlelight Ecstasy Romance®, 1,203,540, is a registered
trademark of Dell Publishing Co., Inc., New York, New York.

ISBN: 0-440-10583-8

Printed in the United States of America

May 1986

10 9 8 7 6 5 4 3 2 1

WFH

To Our Readers:

We have been delighted with your enthusiastic response to Candlelight Ecstasy Romances®, and we thank you for the interest you have shown in this exciting series.

In the upcoming months we will continue to present the distinctive, sensuous love stories you have come to expect only from Ecstasy. We look forward to bringing you many more books from your favorite authors and also the very finest work from new authors of contemporary romantic fiction.

As always, we are striving to present the unique, absorbing love stories that you enjoy most—books that are more than ordinary romance. Your suggestions and comments are always welcome. Please write to us at the address below.

Sincerely,

The Editors
Candlelight Romances
1 Dag Hammarskjold Plaza
New York, New York 10017

THE BITTER
WITH
THE SWEET

CHAPTER ONE

The movie, *"The Beat of Broadway,"* was a wrap. Now, if it did as well at the box office as the play did last year on the stage of the Mark Halper Theater, all the bigshots involved in filming the musical extravaganza would be planning their Oscar acceptance speeches.

Maggie Doyle, the assistant choreographer on *Beat,* was going to be too busy over the next six months to fret about the fact that assistants never get called up to the podium. In any case, she still might get the chance to give her own breathless thanks at New York's Tony Awards. A month earlier, she had landed the job of a lifetime: head choreographer for a new Broadway musical, *Dance Scene,* which was going into rehearsals right after *Beat* was finished.

It had been pure luck, the luck of the Irish, as the red-headed Maggie was wont to say. On the day that Dennis Arcaine, the biggest producer to hit the Great White Way in years, had shown up unannounced at a *Beat* rehearsal on the back lot of Stage Seven, the head choreographer, Chet Castle, was flat on his back with a muscle spasm.

Maggie's tale wasn't exactly that of the understudy who stepped in for the ailing lead and brought down the house, but it was close enough.

Dennis Arcaine watched the tireless, energetic Maggie put her dancers through their paces all afternoon. Fortunately, she had had no idea who he was at the time, having only heard of Arcaine through his reputation. Otherwise, she might have been on her best behavior. As it was, she yelled, stamped her feet, cursed like a truck driver every time someone missed a step, made a dozen changes, and pushed every single one of those dancers, as well as herself, to the breaking point. But when it was time to shoot, the number not only worked, it was perfect. Zeke Harper, the director, declared it the best dance routine he'd ever gotten on film.

The rest was history. Arcaine walked over to Maggie while she was gulping down a soda, handed her his card, told her about *Dance Scene*, and asked the long-legged, red-headed, perspiring assistant if she was interested in being the lead choreographer. When she could finally get her vocal cords to work, Maggie croaked a breathless, "Are you kidding?" She quickly tacked on a long string of yesses and proceeded to spill her half-full bottle of soda all over herself.

Maggie arrived early at the wrap party for *Beat*. She had a plane to New York to catch in an hour and was just dropping in to say her goodbyes. Leaving her suitcase in one of the studio lockers, she ran a comb through her brilliant red hair and rummaged in her purse for a string of

10

pearls to dress up her black linen traveling suit. The catch on the pearl choker was broken. She tossed the necklace back into her purse, adjusted the cowel neck on her royal blue silk blouse, and remembered just in time to switch from the low-heeled pumps she always favored to a more festive pair of spiked sandals.

Maggie knew, dressy shoes or not, that she was likely to be the most underdressed person in the place, but she wouldn't have time to change before leaving for the airport. Besides, appearances had never concerned the lithe Maggie Doyle. In her own estimation, her lanky dancer's figure served merely as a clothes hanger; she was far more concerned with how her body moved and worked than with what it looked like. Dance had been the focus of Maggie's life since she was nine years old taking ballet with Helga Swindlan in a chilly, cavernous dance studio in Peoria, Illinois.

None of the big names had arrived at the party yet; each of them was no doubt planning his or her big entrance. But all the extras, the chorus line, the stagehands, the "little people," as Maggie jokingly called them, were already on hand, getting their fill of champagne and eating fancy hors d'oeuvres that looked a lot prettier than they tasted.

The dancers gathered around Maggie, eager to wish her good luck in New York and let her know there were no hard feelings for the way she had worked their bodies to death.

"It was worth every charley horse, Mag," Steve Ward teased. "Even if I never walk again,

11

I'll be able to say I once worked with the famous Maggie Doyle."

"Only famous?" Maggie turned her big green eyes on him. "What about infamous?"

Elana Young, a pretty blond dancer dressed in sparkling metallic lamé, grinned. "Sorry, Maggie, you have a long way to go for that kind of rep. Ask our star, Hallie Michaels, for lessons in infamy. Now *she* knows how to get headlines in *Inside World*, the sleaziest rag on the newsstands."

"You're all work and no play, Maggie. How do you expect to build up gossip points that way?" Cole Leonard's deep blue eyes lingered on her heart-shaped face. No one missed the shadow of disappointment in the dancer's look.

"True," Maggie said with a soft smile, "but if I hadn't been all work, I wouldn't be catching a plane in an hour for Broadway."

"Broadway," Wes Newman injected laconically. "What's the big deal?"

"No big deal," Maggie agreed blithely. "Unless, of course, your entire life depends on it."

"How is Chet taking it? Still as gracious as ever about your big break?" Rocky Farrell quipped.

"Let's be fair, folks," Maggie said with a devilish smile. "Arcaine did fly out here to see Chet at work. It was pure Irish luck that he was out sick that day."

"Ah, Maggie me girl, the leprechauns sure and begorra are lookin' after you. I doubt the renowned Chet Castle feels very lucky right about now." Georgia Allen's Irish brogue had a distinctly Southern lilt to it.

Everyone laughed, at the same time reaching out for more champagne as a newly filled tray breezed by, carried by a gorgeous would-be starlet who was doing waitress duty until she got discovered.

Maggie checked her watch. "Well, folks, you know the saying, the show must go on." She did a nifty little step-shuffle-kick routine and threw kisses.

"Not waiting for the lords and ladies to arrive on the set?"

Maggie grinned. "I'm simply one of the commoners, remember? Listen, I better see some of you at tryouts next week. Break open your piggy banks and hitch a ride to New York, folks. I'll need a few dancers on that Broadway stage who've come to know and love the Doyle method of dance."

"Some of us have another name for that method of yours, Mag," Cole said, regaining his equanimity, "but I can't say it in mixed company."

"Come on, you loved every minute of it," she teased, then swallowed hard. It was a bad phrase to say to a man who'd made every attempt possible to win her away, if only for a brief while, from stage and screen.

"I better hit that yellow brick road if I plan to board that plane." She looked around at the dancers who'd worked so hard and done so well. Oh, they'd griped and bitched, but they had come through with shining colors. "What can I say?" Maggie smiled wistfully. "You're all real troupers, in the finest sense of the word. It's been swell."

Elana hugged her. "You're going to knock 'em dead on Broadway, Maggie."

Everyone agreed. Maggie squinted to stop any wayward tears as Cole edged the others out of the way.

"Do you need a lift?" he asked.

"Thanks, but I called a cab. It should be waiting outside the main gate."

"I'll walk with you." He followed her and waited while she got her suitcase, then carried it outside for her.

Roy, the old security guard who must have been at Paradyne Studios since they first opened their doors, flicked the switch on the automatic gate. Maggie blew him a kiss.

"That must be my cab," she said, glancing over at a dented yellow taxi. The driver was leaning against the fender, holding an expensive-looking camera with a telephoto lens.

Cole leaned over and kissed her. It was a light peck, since Maggie was giving off her standard keep-your-distance hint, a friendly message but a firm one.

When Cole looked over at the cab, he stopped short. "What the hell is he doing?" he said, just as the driver turned in their direction and snapped a photograph.

Maggie grinned. "He's probably your typical stargazer. Must think we're already famous."

"Hollywood." Cole shook his head. Then he pulled Maggie to him, forgetting about her "message" for the moment. He swept his arms around her, kissing her the way he'd wanted to for months. When he released her, he whispered huskily, "Break a leg, Mag."

Which is exactly what she did.

The minute Maggie Doyle stepped into that battered yellow cab and told the driver her destination, she had this weird premonition. Maybe, she thought, it was because in all the years she'd gotten in and out of taxis, she'd never met a cabbie like Hank August.

"Boyfriend?" he asked as he pulled away from the curb.

"Excuse me?" Maggie's voice was curt.

"You're breaking his heart. There he stands, forlorn, fighting back the tears, watching you fade into the sunset." Hank August glanced into his rearview mirror. "Oh, there he goes, head bent, moving slowly—"

"Are you rehearsing for a movie or writing one?"

Hank turned his head. "What's the matter? Doesn't his pain get to you at all? You don't look like one of those cold-hearted women."

"Would you mind keeping your eyes on the road? I'd like to get to the airport in one piece. And he's not my boyfriend."

"Not for want of trying. Give me your address, and I'll send you a copy of the two of you kissing. It will prove my point."

15

Maggie had to laugh. "You've got a new approach, I'll have to hand you that."

Hank August shrugged. "I just thought you'd like the shot for your scrapbook."

"I gave that kind of scrapbook up in my teens. Hey, why are you pulling over?"

"Will you look at that old woman? Fantastic." He pointed his camera through the open window and snapped an elderly bag lady rummaging through a trash can. She looked up and grinned as she spotted Hank's camera. Then she struck an exaggerated pin-up pose, revealing her toothless smile and shredded, baggy hose. Hank got that one for posterity, too.

"Thanks, sweetheart." He waved, pulling back into the Sunset traffic.

"Do you do this kind of thing all the time?" Maggie asked archly.

"All the time? No, but often enough. I have this theory about the senses. You see—"

"Do you think you could concentrate on driving? You're obviously the last of the Renaissance men, artist, poet, philosopher, but I have a plane to catch. Maybe you could save your theories for the next passenger you pick up?"

Hank August shrugged and managed to keep silent for all of five minutes. Maggie wondered if that was a record.

"Let me ask you a question."

"Only if you don't turn around again," Maggie said wearily.

"Of all the senses—sight, touch, taste, smell,

sound—which do you pay the most attention to and which do you pay the least?"

Maggie leaned forward slightly. "Let me give you a friendly piece of advice. You ought to start cultivating a sixth sense—intuition. Because if you did, you'd know intuitively when someone sitting in the back seat of your cab is completely uninterested in having this kind of conversation."

"You're a dancer, right?"

"How did you know that?"

"Intuition."

Maggie laughed. She hated to give in, but she couldn't help herself.

Hank pulled over and turned to snap a photo of her. Her laugh vanished instantly. "Dammit. Stop doing that. Anyway, I'm a choreographer, not a dancer."

"You have a great face. Especially when your muscles aren't all drawn and tensed. You ought to relax more. Which is part of my theory of the five—excuse me, six—senses."

"Oh, God, not that again."

"You see, the thing is, most of us don't really feed our senses enough."

"Starving senses," Maggie said with as much sarcasm as she could.

"Terrific! I love that phrase." Managing the wheel with one hand, Hank plucked a small notebook and pen from his visor and jotted it down.

"Are you married?"

Hank turned again to glance back at her. "Are you proposing?"

17

Maggie cast her eyes up to the roof of the cab.

"No, really, you probably won't believe this, but I've had two proposals of marriage right in this cab." He chuckled. "One was from a guy, so I usually don't count that. But the other was from this real dish. She looked a little like a young Marilyn Monroe and had this great Zsa Zsa Gabor accent. She told me I looked a lot like a young Burt Reynolds before he grew the moustache and lost his hair."

"A match made in heaven. How Hollywood."

"Well, it turned out not to be love at first sight. Her visa was about to expire, and she needed an American husband, pronto."

"You must have been devastated when you learned the truth. I hope you found out before the wedding."

"I would have helped her out, only my divorce wasn't final then. Which answers your question. I was married for eleven years. Divorced for three. So I am available." He started to turn around to face Maggie again, but spotting her frown, he settled for grinning at her through the rearview mirror.

"I only asked because I would have sent a letter of commiseration to your wife—after I finished writing a grievance letter to your cab company."

"Well, I just saved you a piece of fancy stationery. Really, two. See this?" He tapped a finger on his posted license. "Independent cabbie. I'm my own boss. You can write to me, though. Maybe we could be pen pals."

"I don't—"

"I know. You gave that up when you were a kid. Which leads to another theory of mine."

"Do you torment all your passengers this way?"

"What's the matter, sweetie? Got a problem? Tell old Hank all about it."

"I do not believe you. The only problem I have is finding myself in your taxi. In fact, I have the world at my feet. Things couldn't be going better." She paused, her brows arching. "I know. This is Candid Camera, right? You're putting me on, and I'm going to make a total ass of myself on TV."

"I think that show went off the air. Now, that was a great program. People captured in a moment of truth. That's what my photography is all about. Hey, don't blow a fuse," he said suddenly, pulling over again.

"No. Don't you dare—"

But it was too late. Hank was already focusing his camera on one of Hollywood's colorful punkers, this one with a shocking pink Mohawk, an Op Art shirt, and a pair of bright green pants. Maggie wasn't sure whether she was looking at a male or a female. Maybe the punker wasn't so certain either. Anyway, he/she was too busy sharing a bottle of Ripple with a skid-row drunk to ponder gender.

"Did you see the way that kid wiped off the lip of the bottle before taking a slug? God, I hope I got that shot in time." Hank turned around. "You did blow a fuse, huh?"

19

"If I thought there was a chance in hell of finding myself another cab in time, I'd be out of here before you could say cheese."

His hands went to his camera.

"If you take a shot of me now, Mr. August, I guarantee that camera will end up in pieces— after I smash it over your head."

Hank grinned. "I was just about to tuck it into my glove compartment to make you feel better. I promise I'll get you to the airport on time. No more pictures. I'll even spare you my theory about life's little kindnesses and how they can go a long way." He pulled the cab back onto the road and picked up his speed.

"I assume that was a direct attack."

"No. No, it wasn't. There are certain kinds of people who find me irritating."

"The ones who aren't gay or about to be deported?"

Hank laughed. "You've got a sharp Irish tongue, lass. You also work too hard. I can see it in your face, despite that beautiful rose-petal complexion. You may think things have never been better for you, but deep down you know you're missing out on a lot of life's small gifts."

"You're nuts."

"See what I mean? You gave yourself away by answering so fast."

"And I suppose you're not missing out on any of life's gifts."

"I'm working on it, every day. You might call it my personal quest. Life's short, M.D. What do the initials stand for?"

20

"My luggage, right?"

"You must have guessed by now that I'm a very observant cabbie. So what is it—Maureen, Maura, Margaret?"

"It's none of your business."

"Okay, M.D. Jeez, look at this traffic. Half of L.A. must be catching a plane tonight."

"Maybe if you hadn't stopped so many times to capture those real moments on thirty-five-millimeter film, we might have missed some of this mess. I'm going to end up taking a later plane at this rate—if there *is* another flight leaving for New York tonight. Maybe you ought to get off the freeway and try the side roads."

Ignoring her suggestion, he asked, "What's the big prize in New York?"

"Look, I think if you get off at the next exit and get onto Mission, we'll do a lot better."

"I don't think you're right, M.D."

"Don't keep calling me that. It's Maggie, okay? Now, since I'm the one paying for this ride, how about doing what I say and take that exit? I've taken Mission before, and it usually moves faster."

"You're the boss, Maggie. Maggie. Yeah, I like that. Suits you." He pulled off at the Jude Street exit and turned left onto Mission.

"See, what did I tell you? It's much less crowded," she said.

Hank pulled up at a red light. "I guess you're right, Maggie. Never let it be said that Hank August didn't pay his due respects. Smart lass."

"Thanks," she said with a begrudging smile. As

21

infuriating as Maggie found Hank August, she had to admit he was definitely one of a kind. She also had to admit that he did look like a young, handsome Burt Reynolds with his dark hair, ruggedly masculine features, and broad shoulders. There was even something special in the tone of his voice.

"You still didn't tell me why you're dashing off to New York City. A job? Definitely not a guy."

"Intuition?"

Hank laughed. "So what's this great job you landed?"

"Just the head choreographer in an Arcaine production. Broadway, here I come."

"Dennis Arcaine, huh? Hey, you did hit the big time. You must be quite a choreographer."

"How do you know about Arcaine? Don't tell me. Another frustrated actor."

"Me? Nah. I don't like memorizing other people's lines, playing parts in other people's stories. I have—"

"A theory, right?"

"Right."

They both laughed. Maggie leaned back in her seat. They were less than ten minutes from the airport, there was very little traffic, and she let herself relax a little. "You ought to write down your theories, Mr. August. I bet your book would end up on the best-seller list."

"Hank. And I'm afraid that's just what would happen."

"You don't want to write a best seller?"

"Success corrupts, Maggie. Every time. You

start by thinking you can handle it, and when you finally realize you can't manage it any more than the next guy, it's too late. Once you buy into making it, you automatically sell out."

"I couldn't disagree more. People need goals, they need to strive for something. Look at that bag lady or that punker you photographed. That's where you end up when you give up trying to be successful."

"Look at me," Hank said.

"I was trying to be tactful. But since you brought it up, okay. Look at you. Is being a cab driver all you want out of life? You seem reasonably intelligent, you're certainly verbal, curious, you obviously enjoy philosophy and photography. Don't tell me you don't have dreams."

"Now you're changing the topic of our discussion. We're talking success, not dreams. Your problem is that you see my being a cab driver as my whole identity. I am therefore I am." He turned to her with a quick wink. "A touch of my personal interpretation there. Anyway, being a cab driver is simply one part of my life. It gives me pocket money and a chance to meet interesting people, expound my theories. I don't have a boss on my back, I don't have a real or invisible time clock to punch. I'll tell you something, Maggie. Once you have success, you have fear, with a capital F, fear of losing it. That's the other sure side of the coin. Now me, I don't have to worry about that."

"Well, once I make it, I'll deal with the other side of the coin. At this moment, I'll settle for choreographing the best damn musical to hit Broadway. You asked me before about which sense is the most important to me? The answer is taste. I want to taste success so bad it hurts. And I'll tell you something else, Socrates. I don't scare very easily."

"Maybe not, but you're missing out on a lot, Maggie."

"Really? Like what?"

"Like love."

"We're not all diehard romantics, Mr. August."

"Hank. And I'm not only talking romance. I'm talking love—brotherly love, love of nature, love of the sights, sounds, aromas, and textures of life, Maggie. Romance isn't enough. Not that it isn't terrific. I love romance."

"But you wouldn't want to strive for it. Then you'd have to start worrying about losing it." She gave him a sardonic smile.

Hank grinned. "Good. You're getting the hang of it. Absolutely. Things like that ought to just happen. The important thing is that you have to be receptive. Now you, you shut yourself off, Maggie. I saw it when your boyfriend kissed you."

"He isn't my boyfriend. And I don't shut myself off. I happen to date fairly often. And I've had a few—romances in my day. A couple of serious relationships, if you want to know."

Hank angled the rearview mirror so he could see her better. "Oh? Look at the way you're sitting right this minute. Arms crossed over your chest, fingers clenched, neck muscles straining.

24

Body language, Maggie. It speaks its own tongue. Your body is telling me—"

"I've really had it with your theories, if you don't mind." She dropped her hands down to her lap and then, angry that she had allowed him to make her feel so self-conscious and so transparent, crossed them back over her chest. She closed her eyes for a few moments, telling herself that it was ridiculous to let this absolute stranger get to her like this.

"There you go. Nice deep breaths, now. Let those muscles go limp. I bet relaxation therapy would do you a world of good."

Maggie glared at the back of his head. "What would do me a world of good, Mr. August, is to step out of this taxi at the airport terminal and slam this door behind me. And if I ever happen to be in this town again and have the misfortune to hail your cab, do me a favor and just drive right on by."

"I hate ending our brief encounter with hard feelings, Maggie. I like you. You just need to expand your outlook, and not let the little things in life get to you."

Maggie had to squeeze her hands together to keep from slugging him. In a tight, brittle voice, she said, "Turn down the next block. It's a shorter route to the airport."

"The one after would be better."

"This one."

Hank shrugged and turned left.

Maggie didn't pay much attention to the blue Chevy at first, not until it came closer and the driver started to weave a little. He had his high beams on, even though the sun hadn't yet set.

"What's the matter with that guy?" Maggie asked sharply as Hank beeped his horn a couple of times.

"Probably drunk." He beeped again. "Come on buddy. Move over—"

The driver of the Chevy, suddenly realizing what was happening, swerved sharply to the right.

Later, Hank figured that the guy must have stepped down on the gas when he meant to hit the brake. At the time, all Hank knew was that the driver started to lose control of the car and in his panic not to slam into the sidewalk, he turned the wheel wildly to the left.

Maggie screamed and threw her hands over her face as she saw the blue car coming straight at them. There was a deafening sound of metal crunching and glass shattering. Then silence.

It was dark. Maggie felt herself moving through space. Odd sounds began to filter through her mind—strange sensations took over her body. But she shut them out. The silence returned.

CHAPTER TWO

Maggie's eyes tried to focus. Everything was white, so white it hurt. She preferred the darkness. Yes, that was better.

"Maggie?" Hank moved closer to the bed.

The nurse touched Hank's shoulder lightly. "She'll fade in and out like this for most of the day."

"What does the doctor say about her ankle?"

"You'll have to speak to him, I'm afraid. He should be in sometime this afternoon. How are you feeling?"

Hank's hand went up to the bandage across his forehead. "Just a few scratches. It doesn't seem fair."

"Accidents never are."

Maggie moaned softly, her eyelids fluttering open again. Hank moved closer to her.

She stared up at him, a vague, sleepy look in her eyes. "Where . . . am I?"

Hank slipped his hand over hers. "You're going to be fine, Maggie. You're in L.A. General."

"Where—?"

But before he could tell her again, her eyes

closed and she was breathing deeply. Hank pulled up a chair beside her bed. The nurse shrugged.

"Just a few more minutes, only because we don't have a patient in the other bed," she said, gathering up her chart and walking out.

The doctor showed up at three fifteen. Hank was still in Maggie's room.

"I thought I sent you home this morning. How's your head?"

Hank shrugged. "It's okay." He stood up. "She came to a few times."

"She'll be fairly alert by tonight. It's not her head that's worrying me."

"Her ankle?"

"Well, we'll just have to play the old waiting game. I'm afraid I'll have to ask you to step out- side while I do my exam, Mr. August." He checked his watch. "Visiting hours are almost up anyway."

"I'll hang around in case she comes to again. I'd like to be the one to tell her."

Dr. Harvey Fieldston, young, earnest, and sin- cere, gave Hank an understanding nod. "It wasn't your fault. From what the police said when they brought you both in, the driver of the other car was drunk and plowed right into you."

"Yeah, I know. But somehow I don't think it's going to matter much to Maggie who was at fault. When she sees that cast on her leg, she's going to take it mighty hard. She's a dancer—a choreogra- pher."

"Tough break." The doctor grimaced. "No pun intended."

Hank smiled. "Hey, in this business, you need a sense of humor."

"Your line of work too," Dr. Fieldston said, smiling back.

"What time is it?"

Maggie's soft voice cut through Hank's grogginess. It was nearly ten P.M. He'd wangled permission to stay in her room until the change of shifts.

He bent down to Maggie, brushing away a strand of hair from her cheek. "It's almost ten. How do you feel?"

"Thirsty."

He poured her a glass of water, stuck in a straw, and moved it to her lips.

She took a small sip. "Scotch would taste better."

"I'll see what I can do later."

Maggie closed her eyes again, opening them almost immediately. "Oh, my God—my plane. I must have missed my plane." Panic spread across her face as her mind started to clear up. "That car—oh, no—"

"It's okay, Maggie. You're going to be just fine."

She looked up at Hank. "Where am I? What happened?"

"You're in the hospital. You—"

"Hospital? I've got to get to New York. I can't stay here." She tried to sit up, only to fall back

29

heavily onto the pillow as a searing blaze of heat shot through her head. "My head."

"You bashed it kind of hard against the door. You've been out cold for a while."

It was when the pain in her head subsided a little that she felt the weight around her leg. Her eyes filled with sickening horror as she wrenched the sheet off and stared down at the white plaster cast that went from her ankle up to her knee. "No. . . . No, no, no."

"I'm sorry, Maggie. It's your ankle. The doctor says—"

Maggie stared up at him in disbelief. "No, dammit. This can't be happening to me. Not now. It's some crazy nightmare."

"I—uh—called Arcaine's office this morning and explained—"

"This morning? What do you mean, this morning?"

"You've been here almost twenty-four hours."

Her hands went up to her face. Hank reached out and stroked her arm.

"It's lousy luck. I feel terrible."

Her hands flew at him. "It's your fault. This is all your fault! Get out!"

"Maggie—"

"Get out of here. Do you hear me? Get out!"

The night nurse came rushing in at the sound of the commotion. "What's wrong? What's going on here?"

Maggie was screaming now. "Get him out of here! Get him out!"

Hank nodded to the nurse and walked toward

the door. He took a quick glance back at Maggie, who was now raging while the nurse vainly attempted to soothe her.

Hank was back at the hospital by nine the next morning. He would have been there earlier, but he'd waited for the florist down the street to open.

The receptionist in charge of the visitor's passes was a small, gray-haired lady, tidy in her candy-striped volunteer's jacket. She looked at the bouquet of daffodils and then up at Hank's face, giving him a sympathetic smile. "I'm sorry, Mr. August. I have a notation on Miss Doyle's card that she's not to have any visitors today."

"Oh? Well, how about if I just go up and give these flowers to the floor nurse so she can bring them into Miss Doyle's room?"

"Well, I don't suppose—"

Hank was already on his way to the elevator.

Maggie's bed had been cranked up, and the tray table was positioned over her lap so that she could have her breakfast. She hadn't touched a thing. Her eyes were closed when Hank snuck in.

"You can take the tray away. I'm not hungry." She opened her eyes then. When she saw Hank, she looked like she was going to scream.

"Please," he said softly, "I just wanted to bring you some flowers and find out how you were feeling."

"I told the nurse I didn't want to see you again," she said icily. "Will you just go away?" She let out a weary sigh, then stared at him, her

31

angry features filled now with an anguish she couldn't mask.

"Is there someone I can call? Family? A friend?"

She shook her head. Hank popped the flowers into the water pitcher. Then he walked over to the window. The shades were drawn, and he started to open them.

"Don't."

"Sunlight plays a big role in helping fight off depression."

"Another of your theories?"

Hank smiled. "Sorry." He let go of the curtain cord and leaned against the wall, staring at her. "I wish it had been me. I mean that."

Maggie bit down on her lower lip. She could feel herself trembling. "I'm sorry . . . for what I said last night. It all came back to me—how that car went out of control. I—I know there was nothing you could do."

Tears fell down her cheeks and she turned her face toward her pillow.

Hank walked over to her bed. "I wish there was something I could do for you," he said tenderly.

"I just want to be left alone. You're absolved, Mr. August. It wasn't your fault. You're not responsible, so just forget it. I don't want your visits. I don't want—" She clenched her jaw, squeezing her eyes shut, refusing to let herself break down.

When she looked over at the window again, Hank hadn't moved. She shook her head slowly.

32

"What is it with you, August? Do you need a bomb to drop on you to get the message?"

"I'm picking up a different message."

For a few minutes, she didn't say anything. Then she asked in a low, sad voice, "How's your head?"

"Just a cut."

"And the other driver—was he—"

"Not even a scratch. His car doesn't look too good, though."

"What about your cab?"

"It needed some body work anyway."

She stared down at her hands. "What did you tell them at Arcaine's office?"

Hank walked over and sat down in the chair beside her bed. "I explained that you'd been in a car accident. Arcaine was very sympathetic. And very disappointed."

"I don't suppose he said anything about delaying the rehearsals for a few weeks." The flash of hope in her eyes vanished before she met Hank's gaze. "No, I didn't think so. He probably called Chet Castle the minute he got off the phone with you."

Hank looked down at her untouched breakfast. He buttered both of the rolls and poured out a cup of coffee. "Milk or sugar?"

"What do I do now?" She stared blankly at him as he held the cup out to her.

"You sit up and share this breakfast with me."

Maggie watched him chew on one of the rolls. "I suppose you take a very philosophic approach to all this. Something like, it was meant to be. Or, go with the flow, or—look on the bright side."

"I'd be mad as hell." He took a sip of her coffee. "And scared." His eyes rested on her face. "Just like you." He walked to the door. "See you at lunchtime."

Maggie closed her eyes after he left, a glimmer of a smile curving her lips. How foolish of her to think she could second-guess the irreverent Hank August. He *would* have to show her compassion and understanding just when she wanted to keep her feelings clearly focused on rage and despair. But despite her determined effort to hold on to those uncomplicated feelings, Hank had managed to touch her—and confuse her even more. It was just like the man, she thought ruefully, but the smile remained for a little while longer.

When Hank arrived back at twelve thirty that afternoon, the nurse's aide was outside Maggie's door, the untouched lunch tray in her hands.

Hank took it from her. "Why don't I see if I can get her to eat something?"

"Go away," Maggie said as he walked in, set the food on the table, and wheeled it back to her bed.

The window curtain was still drawn. Hank ignored her protests and pulled it open, flooding the room with bright sunlight. Maggie felt around for the emergency buzzer, but Hank returned to the bed and removed it from her grasp before she could push it. Then he cranked her up to a near-sitting position.

"Now, let's see what we've got for lunch today," he said cheerily.

"If this is the only way you can get your meals, I'll give you a few bucks to go buy your own."

"Turkey," he said, taking a bite. "Not bad. You want some salt on the potatoes? Salt's lousy for you, but I'll spare you my discourse on its evils—today." He sprinkled a little on the potatoes despite the fact that Maggie refused to say a word. "Pepper? I'm crazy about pepper. A kingly spice. Do you mind?" He tore open the little packet and proceeded to shake half of it over the entire plate of food.

Maggie glared at him. "I hate pepper."

"You should have spoken up."

"Why are you torturing me?"

"Don't get upset. I'll eat the top part and you can have the stuff underneath."

"That's not what I'm talking about, and you know it," she said through clenched teeth, making a grab for the plate. She would have sent it careening across the room if Hank weren't holding it as well.

"Let me eat a little before you do that."

She released her grip on the plate, pressing her hand to her head. "What have I ever done to deserve this?"

"It's okay to feel sorry for yourself."

"How kind of you to give me permission."

Hank grinned, cutting up a piece of the turkey and popping it into his mouth. "For today. By tomorrow, I want to see a little of that sparkle back in your lovely green eyes."

35

"I don't expect to see you here tomorrow. In fact, I don't expect to be here myself."

"Dr. Fieldston already told me you're stuck in this place for three more days. Do you want me to get you some books? Magazines? How about a TV?"

"I just want to be left alone, but I don't suppose that makes any difference to you."

"Oh, before I forget, I stopped by at your apartment this morning. I guess I should say Donna Hamlin's apartment now. She explained that you'd sublet it to her for six months."

"How did you know about the apartment in the first place?"

"I gave Paradyne Studios a call."

"Oh, God, now the word will get around like wildfire. All I need on top of this is to stare at a roomful of pitying faces."

"I thought you might say that, so I didn't give out any details. Anyway, Donna said you could stay with her until you made other plans."

"In a studio apartment that's about the same size as this room?"

"She wasn't real enthusiastic about the idea, either. I told her not to worry about it."

"Terrific. Now only I have to worry."

"I have a theory about worrying—and if you don't watch out, I'll spring it on you."

Maggie managed to eat a little dinner that night. She was surprised when Hank August didn't show up to share it with her. Maybe he didn't like Salisbury steak. Or maybe he was busy explaining his crazy theories to someone else over dinner. She had to admit she was a little disappointed, if only because he made her so mad it took her mind off her misery.

Where were those leprechauns now? she wondered. Her chance of a lifetime, and she had to put her best foot foward into the wrong taxicab. She could forget about Broadway for a while. Well, Chet Castle had just inherited her Irish luck.

There was a light rap on her door. Not Hank August, Maggie thought. He didn't believe in knocking. She prayed it was no one from Paradyne. Hank had promised he'd kept her whereabouts unknown. She was still too steeped in self-pity to handle commiseration from anybody else.

"Come in."

"Oh, good. You're awake." The voice was very deep, startling considering that it came from a diminutive woman who had to be seventy if she was a day. She was dressed in a replica of a suit Maggie remembered seeing in old sepia photos of her great aunts, right down to the starched white high-neck blouse replete with lace trim and a cameo pin. The only thing missing was the bustle in the back of the black gabardine skirt.

The woman smiled. Maggie thought she must have once been very beautiful. Her face, despite the network of wrinkles, was still full of grace and character. Maggie had never seen her before in her life. She figured the woman had come to the wrong room.

The woman stuck her head out the door. "Oscar, come along. Miss Doyle is up." She turned back to Maggie. "He's so slow." Her head disappeared for another instant. "Do hurry, Oscar."

Oscar, a good head and a half taller and at least forty years younger than the elderly woman, appeared at the doorway. He was incredibly thin, the kind of thin that made the tightly pulled belt around his waist vitally important. His skin was slightly pockmarked, either from an adolescent case of acne or from a bad bout of chicken pox. Yet there was something sweet and gentle about his face, an engaging, childlike expression and large, tender brown eyes. He walked in slowly, carrying an armload of shopping bags.

"Where should I set them, Miss May?"

"Let's be neat and tidy, Oscar. We'll stack the books nicely on Miss Doyle's bedside table."

Oscar smiled shyly at Maggie as he moved to the table with the package of books. Maggie, feeling utterly bewildered, merely smiled back. She had no idea who these two odd characters were or why they'd come laden with gifts. Then she caught the label on one of the books Oscar was tidily stacking: *Live Happy and Salt-free*.

"Hank August," Maggie muttered, watching Miss May unpack a grocery bag of health food treats.

"What was that, dear?" Miss May asked, looking for appropriate spots to store the goodies.

"You're friends of Mr. August, aren't you?"

Oscar grinned. Miss May checked Maggie's water pitcher. "Do get Miss Doyle some fresh water, Oscar. Go ask the nurse for some ice as well." She smiled at Maggie. "Of course we're his friends. Oh, Hank had us bring something else for you." She dug deep into her large, old-fashioned black purse and brought out a lavishly gift-wrapped package. "Amy wrapped it."

Of course, Maggie had no idea who Amy was, but she didn't even bother to ask at this point. In fact, this whole encounter had such a strange feeling of fantasy about it that Maggie wondered if she wasn't in the throes of an hallucination caused by her injury. But then she opened the package.

It was an exquisite gilt-edged antique frame. Inside was the photo Hank had taken of her laughing in his cab. She looked at the picture of the carefree, exuberant woman for a long moment, then set it face down on the bed.

"Don't you like it, dear? I thought you looked very lovely. And so happy."

"I had a lot to be happy about when this was taken," Maggie said sullenly, reality hitting her with its full impact again.

Miss May patted her hand sympathetically. "Do you know, I once sang on Broadway. In nineteen twenty-eight, to be exact. It was a thrill —really, quite a thrill. But it was only one of many marvelous experiences in my life. When we lose one opportunity for happiness, a new and often better one will take its place if we allow it."

"Do you tutor Mr. August or does he tutor you?" Maggie asked sarcastically. Then, immediately sorry for behaving so rudely to the sweet old lady, she started to apologize.

But Miss May laughed. "Henry Collier August is a remarkable person, Maggie. I can't tell you what that boy means to me. What he means to all of us."

"All of you?"

"I know I can speak for Oscar, Amy, Timothy, Rita—why, just everyone. You'll see."

Maggie stared up at her blankly. While she was trying to decide whether or not she really wanted any more details about Hank August's fan club, Oscar reappeared with the water pitcher.

"Would you like a glass?" he asked, a bit less awkward now, the same sweet smile on his face.

Maggie didn't have the heart to say no. Oscar handed her the plastic mug filled with fresh ice water, and Miss May opened a box of dried apricots and handed her one.

"Please, help yourselves to something. It was very thoughtful of Mr. August to send you with all of this food and these books," Maggie said.

"Oh, the magazines, Oscar. Don't forget to stack up the magazines. Hank sent you a varied assortment. He thought that whatever you didn't want, you could donate to some of the other patients."

"Yes. Yes, I will."

Miss May lifted the frame from the bed and placed it upright on the bedside table. As she studied it, she smiled.

"Very lovely." She turned to Maggie, taking

her hand. "I've known disappointment in my life —some terrible disappointment. We do understand how terribly unhappy you feel right now. You must love dance."

"It's even more than just the dancing. It's the choreography, the whole creation of movement, giving it form, power. There's nothing more exciting—"

She stared up at Miss May with frightened eyes. "Every time the doctor walks in here, I get this terrible feeling that he isn't sure my ankle will mend properly. He's mentioned that I might need surgery if the cast doesn't work. Miss May, if I had to give up dance, life would be meaningless for me. I know people say that and don't really mean it, but there's nothing in this world I've ever wanted or given my heart to that didn't have to do with dance."

Maggie had never cried against a stranger's shoulder. But as Miss May put her frail, thin arms around her, patting her gently on the top of her head, Maggie sobbed like a baby.

Finally, cried out and exhausted, Maggie fell back onto her pillow. Miss May put a cool hand on her brow and nodded to Oscar, who pulled out a shiny silver flute from yet another shopping bag. As Maggie closed her eyes, Oscar played a soft, lilting tune while Miss May sang. It was an old Irish folksong that Maggie had heard years ago. There was something magical about the duet. As she drifted off, Maggie felt certain that Miss May and Oscar must have stepped out of a dream after all.

Hank was sitting beside her when she awoke the next morning. She squinted in the bright light.

"What time is it? What day is it?" She rubbed her eyes, then saw the books and magazines on her bedside table. The opened box of dried apricots was sitting on top of the small metal bureau. "Miss May and Oscar are real?"

Hank chuckled. "Miss May said you looked too pale. She ordered me to get you out to the sunroom today. But I have a better plan. How would you like to go home?"

"Home?"

"I just spoke to Dr. Fieldston. He said your head is as good as new, and if you practice on your crutches this morning I can take you out of here before we have to suffer through another hospital lunch."

Maggie was thrilled by the prospect of getting out of there, but she was not altogether sure just where she would go. Hank was already rummaging through her suitcase.

He held up a pale blue and white print cotton dress. "How about this?"

"Hank, I have to make some plans, figure out what I'm going to do and where I'll stay."

"It's all been taken care of." He tossed her dress over the chair. "I'll be back in a few minutes."

He was out the door before Maggie could argue.

A perky young nurse-in-training arrived with a

42

pair of wooden crutches as Maggie sat up at the edge of the bed watching the room spin slowly.

"Easy does it. You'll get your bearings in a minute," the nurse said, helping Maggie out of bed and steadying her on her crutches.

"It always looks so simple when other people walk around on these things."

"You'll get used to it."

Maggie nodded, her initial elation at moving about fading in the face of having to hobble around like this for weeks. And what was she supposed to do during this time? Fortunately, she'd put aside a little money for a rainy day. Well, this was as rainy as they came, she thought dully. But beyond being financially solvent, the coming months looked bleak. It would take her that long to get back into shape and probably longer still to find work. Oh, she could always get Danny Weeks to take her on as an assistant choreographer in Vegas, but Maggie had hoped after working with the renowned Chet Castle on three films that she'd get some really big breaks. Big breaks—that was a laugh.

The nurse looked over at Maggie. "Are you all right?"

Maggie hadn't realized she'd actually laughed out loud. "I'm great. Why shouldn't I be? A crippled, out-of-work choreographer with nothing but time on my hands. Yeah, I feel terrific."

"Hey, you won't have that cast for too long. Really, it isn't so bad."

"Do you mind if I practice in here by myself for a few minutes?"

"Are you sure you don't feel dizzy or anything?"

"I'm fine. Honest. I just want to be alone and get dressed, get myself together."

Hank was approaching Maggie's door when the nurse walked out.

"How's she doing?" he asked.

"Okay." She hesitated. "Well, actually, I think she's pretty down. I had this course in psychology in nursing school, and I think she's going through the first two stages of loss."

"Anger and sadness?"

The nurse brightened. "Right."

"You're very perceptive. But I'll look after Maggie Doyle. She'll be fine."

"You were driving, huh?"

Hank nodded.

"You shouldn't feel responsible. I heard the other guy was soused."

Hank smiled, resting his hands on her shoulders. "Being at fault has nothing to do with caring about somebody, feeling a desire to help them."

The pretty young blonde blushed, her big blue eyes lingering on Hank's ruggedly handsome face. Then she looked down at the camera around his neck. "Are you a photographer?"

He grinned. "I'm a feeder of starving senses."

He walked into Maggie's room, leaving the nurse staring after him, a bewildered expression on her face.

Maggie was walking over to the window. She

pivoted around when she heard Hank's foot-
steps.

"Hey, this isn't so hard," she said with a brave
smile, having decided to keep her misery to herself.

Hank snapped her picture. As the flash hit her
eyes, she smiled ruefully. "Dammit, I wish you
wouldn't keep doing that."

He got that picture, too.

CHAPTER THREE

Maggie stopped dead in her tracks outside the hospital entrance as she saw a chauffeur open the passenger door of a vintage black Bentley, glistening like brand-new patent leather in the late morning sun. She took a quick look over her shoulder, expecting to see some big-name celebrity behind her. But there was no one else around. She eyed Hank suspiciously.

"Don't tell me this is what you rented while your cab is getting its dents removed."

Hank smiled. "It's Timothy's."

"Timothy?" Then she remembered Miss May mentioning the name Timothy—another of Henry Collier August's fans.

Hank guided her over to the elegant automobile.

"Hutch, this is Maggie Doyle. Maggie, meet Timothy Randolph Hutchins, driver to the stars. Everyone from Charlie Chaplin to Joan Crawford. Ten years with Paula Wilton, the silent-screen star." He leaned closer to Maggie, whispering, "She asked him to marry her, but Hutch felt it wouldn't be quite proper."

"Delighted," Timothy Hutchins said with a regal British accent. The chauffeur was a very small man, his face deeply etched with wrinkles, his hair a pure white. He had a slight tremor but otherwise looked very spry. He was dressed in the standard crisp black uniform, starched white shirt, and black tie. Upon greeting Maggie, he immediately placed his brimmed hat neatly under his arm and bowed slightly from the waist.

Maggie was taken aback when the rather formal chauffeur suddenly winked at Hank and chuckled. "You overlooked mentioning to Miss Doyle that Paula Wilton was a good twenty years my senior. It wouldn't have worked on all counts, I'm afraid. She finally married Frederick Elgin, the oil magnate. I continued driving her for six months after that. Then her husband got nervous." He gave Maggie a sly grin. "Had cause, he did. The woman never could get over me. Left me the old Bentley in her will." He patted the roof of the car lovingly.

Maggie smiled. "It's a beauty."

"Shall I, miss?" Timothy reached for her crutches.

Hesitating, she looked over at Hank. "You haven't even given me a chance to sort out where I'm going to stay. I suppose you could give me a lift back to my apartment. I can squeeze in with Donna for a couple of days until I decide—"

"Miss May has a room all ready for you," Hank said, taking hold of one of her crutches.

Maggie gripped it tighter. "Hold on. I can't do that."

"Oh, and I forgot to mention she's making a special lunch for you. Been busy at it all morning."

"It smelled divine," Timothy piped in.

"Oh, do you live with Miss May?"

"In a manner of speaking." He chuckled.

"Hutch rents a room on the second floor. Miss May runs a boardinghouse in Venice." Hank rested his hand on the rung of her crutch. "It's all very proper. Come on. If we're late, she'll have my head."

"I suppose you live there as well?"

"It's the best place in town. Right on the canal, soft Pacific breezes drifting by, fine food, homey, and easy on the wallet. You'll love it."

"I'll go for lunch. After that, we'll see." Maggie relented, letting go of the crutches and allowing Hank to help her onto the plush burgundy leather backseat.

Hank slid open the glass partition separating them from Timothy Hutchins.

"Do we pick Oscar up on the way?"

"No. Rita went by for him earlier."

"Doesn't Oscar live in the rooming house too?" Maggie asked as Hutch pulled out slowly into the traffic.

"Oscar visits often, but he lives at the Santa Lucia Institution. Miss May has been doing volunteer work there for years, and Oscar has become very special to her. It was Miss May who discovered he had remarkable musical ability. She bought him the flute."

48

"He plays wonderfully. How long has he taken lessons?"

"Oscar has never had a lesson. He can't read. And with the exception of Miss May and very few others, Oscar won't speak." Hank gave Maggie a tender look. "You must have made quite an impression on him."

"Me?"

"He's composed a new tune especially for you. He's going to play it after we have lunch."

Maggie flushed with pleasure. "I'm—really touched."

"See what you might have missed if fate hadn't intervened?"

"I hate to disappoint you, but I would rather have gotten onto that plane in one piece—even if Oscar were Chopin reincarnated. Do you have any idea how rare it is for a twenty-nine-year-old woman to be asked by someone like Arcaine to choreograph a Broadway show? I've spent endless hours every day for a good twenty of those years preparing for that opportunity. And I might live to be a hundred without getting a second shot at it."

"What have you done besides dance for the last twenty years?" Hank asked.

Maggie narrowed her eyes. "Something tells me that question is a setup for you to lay one of your inimitable theories of life on me."

Hank laughed. "I like you, Maggie Doyle."

"Do I hear a 'but' in there?"

"Oh"—he winked—"you just need a chance to slow down a little and take stock."

"And no doubt you plan to teach me how to do that," she retorted, faintly amused.

"Naturally." He grinned.

"Sorry, but you'd be wasting your time. I don't need to take stock. I know exactly what I want. Let me tell you one of *my* theories, Hank. Life is short. There's no time to waste it frivolously."

"I hate to belabor the point, but you do have a few weeks to kill."

Maggie sighed. "Don't remind me." She looked over at him, the smile replaced by a flash of fear. "I just hope that's all it is. The doctor wants me back for X-rays next week." She paused, staring down at the cast. "When I was working with the Tina Isaacs Modern Dance Troupe a few years ago, one of the dancers broke her ankle in a skiing accident. She must have gone through six operations. It never did mend properly."

"What did she do?"

"She ended up having to choose between staying on as wardrobe mistress or going back home and marrying her high school sweetheart." Maggie glanced over at him. "I went to her wedding."

"Ah, I love a happy ending."

"She was divorced eight months later."

"What would you do?" Hank asked.

"I don't want to have to make that kind of decision," Maggie said firmly. "Anyway, I don't have a high school sweetheart."

"Couldn't fit one in between dance classes?"

"Still can't," she said. "You had me pegged

50

right from the start, Mr. August. I'm a cold-hearted woman in single-minded pursuit of success."

"I'll work on that." He grinned at her.

Maggie rolled her eyes. "Don't you even give down-and-out people a break?"

"They're the ones that need my attention the most." He winked, letting his eyes linger on her.

Feeling herself squirm under his scrutiny, Maggie said, "Don't do that." She looked up and met his gaze.

Somebody honked behind them, making Maggie jump. Timothy Hutchins honked back, ignoring the frustrated driver and continuing to leisurely maneuver the old Bentley down Santa Monica Boulevard.

Hank glanced out the window. "Almost home." He turned back to Maggie, a most disturbing glint in his eyes. "No, I don't think you're cold-hearted."

Maggie broke into a laugh. "You're far too sure of yourself and your theories, Mr. August."

"We'll see," he said with a smile as the Bentley turned down Centinela Avenue into Venice.

In typical Hollywood fashion, this Venice, modeled after its namesake in Italy, was originally built in a lavish fashion, replete with canals and ornate little bridges; it even had gondolas once upon a time. Then the fairy-tale land was abruptly destroyed when oil was discovered in Venice. The oil was soon depleted, and over the past twenty years Venice underwent a rebirth. Some of the old villas and resort properties were bought up and restored, and dozens of restaurants and boutiques sprang up, a sure sign that Venice was back in vogue. Still, much of the area had been left untouched and retained a funky, old-world charm in spite of its somewhat battered appearance.

Timothy Hutchins pulled the Bentley up to the side of an old Victorian house, painted a whimsical pistachio with pale peach trim. The front of the house overlooked one of the canals. Maggie grinned. "It suits you."

Hank laughed. "I'm not sure if that's a compliment or not."

"It's great. I love it."

"Wait until you see your room."

"Not so fast," she said, but Timothy Hutchins was already removing her suitcase from the trunk. Maggie sighed, sticking her crutches under her arms. She didn't argue. After all, she really had nowhere else to go. And, as much as she hated to admit it, there was something about the irrepressible Henry Collier August that intrigued her—as did his friends, Miss May, Oscar, and Hutch.

A bunch of odd ducks, she thought with a smile, charming though, and very sweet. For an only child, who had been raised by reserved, undemonstrative parents in a small, drab apartment in Peoria, Illinois, the notion of being taken into the big sunny home of this effervescent group tugged on Maggie's heartstrings.

When she got to the steep front steps, she found herself suddenly being scooped up into

Hank's strong arms. Timothy Hutchins calmly picked up her dropped crutches and followed after them, both men ignoring her protests. The escalating beat of Maggie's pulse as she was pressed against Hank August's broad chest gave her some strong second thoughts about her tentative decision to spend the next few weeks in the same rooming house as him. A broken ankle was more than enough for her to contend with right now.

"I could have managed on my own," she said curtly as Hank set her down carefully by the front door.

"But it was so much more fun this way," he teased.

"You are impossible," she snapped.

Mr. Hutchins chuckled as he handed her back her crutches. "Don't disturb yourself now, miss. He's a bit of a rogue." He knocked lightly on the stained glass window.

A middle-aged woman with short, fading blond hair and a sharply angular face opened the door. She was dressed in a light blue velour running suit, tube socks, and well-worn royal blue running shoes. Her forehead glistened with sweat, and she was slightly breathless. As Hank introduced Maggie to Rita Lewis, the woman did a few leg stretches in place.

"Rita has the room above yours," Hank said as they moved into the front hall and closed the door.

"Miss May put you on the main floor so you'd be able to get around more easily. The only prob-

53

lem might be the noise from the parlor, but none of my programs start before nine," Rita said between knee bends.

"Programs?" Maggie asked.

"Rita is our resident organizer," Hank said, putting his arm affectionately around the older woman's shoulder. "She just started a fitness program for the over-fifties. She also runs a neighborhood arts and crafts program, a day-care center, and a carpentry workshop. She's always looking for volunteers."

Rita gave Hank an affectionate grimace. "I never coerce."

"Don't believe her," Timothy Hutchins piped in. "She's got me wiping tots' noses two mornings a week."

Hank laughed. "Admit it, Timothy. You're a sucker for those tots and you know it."

"Well, a few of them—just a few—aren't all that bad," Timothy said with a blush.

"He even takes them for drives in his precious Bentley," Rita added, then looked at Maggie pensively, "we might want to think about starting up a dance class now that you're here. Hank told me you were a choreographer."

Maggie gave her cast a rueful glance. "My choreography days are on hold for a while."

"Don't let a little thing like that stop you. We'll work something out," Rita said, full of enthusiasm.

Maggie wished Dennis Arcaine had said that. How ironic to be heading for the Great White Way only to end up choreographing an amateur

54

dance troupe in a slightly rundown rooming house in Venice, California.

Rita moved to resume her leg stretches, nearly getting knocked over as the front door burst open and a young woman flew into the room.

"Oops, sorry." Helping Rita up, the young woman banged into one of Maggie's crutches, knocking it down. She bent to retrieve it.

"And this is Amy Jordan," Hank announced, catching hold of Maggie's arm to steady her.

Amy Jordan looked like she was either on her way to a costume party or else some evil witch had just cast a spell on her. Her hair stood up in spiked points, the tips platinum blond, the rest dark brown. Her makeup looked as if it had been applied with the same paintbrush that had been used to paint the house—maybe with the same paint.

She gave Maggie a breezy "hi," then looked down at her blank white cast. "I can do some great drawings for you on that. After lunch, okay?"

As Maggie was trying to come up with a polite way to turn down the offer, Miss May entered from the parlor. Today she was dressed in an old-fashioned black silk afternoon dress. The same cameo brooch was pinned just below the high neckline.

"Well, then, if we're all here, let's dine, shall we?" Miss May said, giving Maggie a welcoming pat on the shoulder, then smiling affectionately at Amy. "I think I prefer the red to the blond. But this is quite striking."

"Amy sings with Soup," Hank explained as everyone filed down the long hallway. "It's a terrific rock group. They're at a joint in Hermosa Beach for the next couple of weeks. I'll have to take you down to hear them."

Miss May turned. "They're hot," she said, her eyes sparkling.

Maggie smiled politely. Punk rock wasn't her favorite music. Last year she'd worked as an assistant choreographer on a movie about break dancing, and she had gone home every night nursing a splitting headache from the ear-shattering sounds.

Miss May's dining room, unlike the outlandish color scheme on the outside, was decorated in a surprisingly tasteful and subdued pale mauve. An enormous oval-shaped oak table and chairs took up most of the center of the space; a large matching buffet ran along one side of the room. There was a rather threadbare but still lovely Persian rug in rich earth tones covering the wooden floor.

Large blow-ups of photographs adorned every wall in the room. Maggie stopped at the first one, immediately recognizing the bag lady Hank had photographed from the cab. It was a remarkable shot, full of feeling and personality. She walked slowly by some of the other portraits, each equally exciting and rich.

"Did you do all these?" she asked Hank.

"He's wonderful, isn't he?" Rita said. "He has a way of seeing into your soul."

Maggie felt her cheeks redden slightly. She

56

had a disturbing feeling that Rita was right. "They're excellent. Do you ever show your work at galleries?"

"No. Never have," Hank said lightly.

"Well, you should. You're certainly as talented —more talented—than a lot of successful photographers. In fact, I have a friend who owns a gallery in San Francisco. He'd absolutely flip over your work."

Hank led her to a seat, setting her crutches against the wall. "You know my theory about success."

Miss May, Timothy, and Rita all smiled as they joined them around the table.

"I'm afraid you'll never get Henry to go commercial," Miss May said. "He doesn't believe in it."

"Maybe he's just scared," Maggie said, giving Hank a questioning glance.

"I am scared," he admitted. "I'm scared of losing that precious entity called freedom. I take photographs because it gives me pleasure. Once I started doing it for fame and fortune, a lot of the fun would go out of it."

Oscar and Amy carried in the soup, then joined the others at the table. It was the strangest group Maggie could ever remember sitting down to dine with. She felt a little like Alice in Wonderland making a wrong turn and ending up at the Mad Hatter's place in time for tea.

After lunch, Oscar played his tune for Maggie. She had to blink away several tears. Then she noticed Miss May demurely dabbing her eyes, and they shared a smile. Later, everyone went into the parlor and Miss May played the piano, she and Hutch singing a medley of old favorites. Then Hank, not failing in his ability to astonish Maggie, picked up the guitar from the window seat and played a few country and western tunes, crooning along in a husky, sexy voice that sounded like a cross between Willie Nelson and Kenny Rogers. Maggie found her pulse starting to race again.

While everyone joined in to sing with Hank, Maggie hobbled outside and leaned her crutches against the porch railing. She stood on the porch watching a trio of ducks float by on the canal.

"Are you okay?"

Maggie looked over her shoulder at Hank. "You play a mean guitar. Not a bad singing voice, either."

"You know a good agent, right?" He chuckled.

She pivoted around, resting against the porch railing for support. "I think it's a waste. You've got so much talent, Hank."

"What's wrong with that?"

"You know what I mean."

He came closer, resting his hands lightly on Maggie's shoulders. "I went your route once, just took a different path. Oh, I used my talents all right. You would have been proud of me."

Maggie saw the wry smile on his lips but sensed deeper feelings—anger or sadness? She realized that there was more depth to the idiosyncratic Hank August than she had imagined.

"And what route did you take?" she asked.

"I was a kind of traveling salesman." His smile broadened as Maggie's eyes revealed astonishment.

"A traveling salesman? What did you sell?" Maggie was almost afraid to hear the answer.

He squeezed her shoulders lightly. "I sold myself, Maggie. I wandered up and down the highways and byways of Oregon telling people all the reasons why they ought to keep voting for Henry Collier August for state senator."

Maggie grinned. "Now, a politician I can believe. I'm sure you were terrific."

He leaned closer, touching her lips so lightly that Maggie would have been hard put to actually call it a kiss.

"I was terrific," he said, studying her reaction.

"I bet you drove mothers and babies wild," she said, removing Hank's hands from her shoulders. "So what happened?"

Hank observed her thoughtfully. "I was miserable. That was it, plain and simple. I ate, slept, and breathed politics. I was married to the perfect politician's wife, had two perfect politician's children—I even had the perfect politician's father-in-law, Gil Hamilton, once governor of the great state of Oregon. I was being groomed to step into his shoes. But you know what?"

Maggie smiled. "They were the wrong size for your big feet?"

Hank laughed, his hands finding their way back to Maggie's shoulders, his fingers idly caressing her neck. For some reason that Maggie wasn't all that sure of, she didn't protest.

"And he had lousy taste, besides. Wore these fancy black alligator shoes with pointy toes and thick heels."

"I never realized the shoes went with the job."

"Neither did I at first. Or maybe I did, but Lucy, my ex-wife, convinced me I would look great in them. She was bound and determined to move back into the governor's mansion, by hook or by crook."

Maggie picked up the slight inflection on the word *crook*. She started to question him about it, but Hank cut her off most effectively. This time when he moved his lips to hers, there was no doubt in her mind that she was being kissed. He did it very well. Maggie closed her eyes and let her hands slip around his neck.

When she opened her eyes again, her gaze drifted from Hank's languorous smile to the group of people watching the show from the parlor window. Miss May, Hutch, and Rita were smiling, obviously delighted with the performance. Maggie wasn't. She pushed Hank away, and he knocked into her crutches, toppling them over. She bent over, only to lose her balance and find herself once again in Hank's capable arms.

"Let go of me," she snapped. "I'm not interested in a brief fling while I hang around waiting for this damn ankle to heal, especially not with someone like you."

"What's wrong with me?" Hank asked pleasantly.

"What's wrong with you? I'll tell you what's wrong with you. You're an overgrown adolescent

60

who obviously couldn't handle being an adult. So you walked out on your career, your wife, your kids, all the people who believed in you enough to cast their vote your way. I think you're irresponsible, childish, self-involved—" She struggled from his grip, managing to get her crutches. Breathless with anger, she looked up into his eyes. What she saw surprised and disturbed her. She had doubted that her words would have much effect on the cavalier Mr. August, but she was wrong. There was a pained expression on his face that effectively tore the rage out from under her.

"I've thought all those same accusations," he admitted. "I'm sure there's some truth to each of them." With that, he turned away and walked down the steps. Maggie watched him stroll slowly along the canal. She might have gone after him had Miss May not come outside.

"He'll be all right," Miss May said softly. "I often tell Hank his one great fault is that he feels things too deeply. That's why he could never last in politics. I always tell him that it was only a matter of time."

"What went wrong? Why did he quit when he did?" Maggie asked.

Miss May patted her cheek. "He'll tell you himself in time. He likes you, Maggie."

"He seems to like everyone," Maggie said, a flush returning to her cheeks.

"Oh, he has a great capacity for caring, but I've never, in the three years I've known Hank, seen him kiss a woman so passionately. I think, when he and his wife separated, he placed that part of his feelings behind a locked door. You, my dear, have clearly provided a key."

Maggie shook her head. "That's not what I intended. I'm not looking for romance, Miss May. My only wish is to get this ankle of mine back in one piece and get on with my career. I'm the wrong kind of person for Hank August. We're like fire and water."

Miss May's eyes sparkled. "Ah, but fire and water can create a great deal of exciting steam. 'Steam Heat.' Peggy Lee sang that song. It was very sexy."

Maggie grinned. "You must have been something in your day."

Miss May winked. "I still manage pretty well."

"Yes, I can see that," Maggie replied with a smile.

Miss May took Maggie's hand. "Your room is ready for you, but perhaps you'd like to relax awhile on the porch. Such a pretty day." Her eyes gazed beyond Maggie to Hank, who was now standing idly at the bank of the canal, throwing stones aimlessly into the water.

Maggie followed Miss May's gaze. "Yes, I think I will stay out here a bit."

Miss May gave Maggie an approving smile and then briskly turned and walked back into the house.

Maggie straightened her crutches and carefully made her way down the front steps. It wasn't an easy task, but she was pleased that she could manage it on her own. The grassy bank of the canal was even trickier, her crutches sinking slightly into the moist earth.

Hank looked up as she drew near. He smiled. "Hey, you're getting good on those sticks."

When Maggie made it to his side, she smiled back, then looked out at the water. "I owe you an apology, Hank. I had no right to attack you like that."

Hank cupped Maggie's chin, tilting her face up to him. "I have a theory about apologies."

Maggie brushed her fiery hair away from her face, her eyes sparkling. "Yes, I bet you do."

CHAPTER FOUR

Maggie awoke to the strange sound of breathless panting. She thought at first that she must be dreaming, but then she remembered it was Thursday. On Tuesdays and Thursdays, Rita conducted her morning exercise class for the over-fifties. Maggie had stepped in to watch for a few minutes on Tuesday. Rita gave her group quite a workout, but the women seemed to be having a grand time. As Maggie observed the class from the doorway that morning, she was sharply reminded of her last days on the *Beat* set, working with her group of dancers. It was only two weeks ago, and yet it felt like a lifetime.

Maggie sat up in bed and pushed the covers off. As she looked down at her cast, she found herself smiling despite the depression that never fully left her. Amy had done quite a job on the white plaster. Doves, rainbows, and whimsical airy creatures of no known name or origin decorated nearly every inch of space. Although Maggie had been reticent, to say the least, about the enterprise, she was glad now that she'd let Amy whisk out her Magic Markers and "do her thing." Maggie far preferred this artistic mélange to the stark, cold-looking, white plaster of paris.

Maggie's two weeks at Miss May's boarding-house had been filled with many surprising and unique experiences. She had discovered, for instance, that Amy's rock group, Soup, who'd come to entertain for an impromptu neighborhood block party—organized, of course, by Rita—were really very good. Amy especially, the lead singer, had a rich, earthy voice that was both sensual and melodic.

One morning, speaking to Amy over breakfast, Maggie learned that both Amy's stint with Soup and her residence at Miss May's had been Hank's doing. Nearly three years ago, at the ripe old age of twenty-one, Amy had been moving along a fast track heading nowhere. The day she got into Hank's cab, she'd finally come to what looked like a dead end. Out of money, hope, and self-respect, Amy told Hank to take her for a long, slow drive up Topanga Canyon. She planned to have him leave her off at the scenic summit, where she intended to bid her final farewell to Hollywood and the world.

"I had enough sleeping pills in my purse to wipe out King Kong," Amy told Maggie. "I was bound and determined not to botch up the job. I was going to slip into perpetual dreamland watching L.A. sparkle in the night."

"And Hank guessed what you were up to?" Maggie asked.

Amy grinned. "Guessed? Honey, he practically named the doctor I'd wangled the prescription out of. He had my number down so well, it freaked me out. Before I knew what was happening, he was making a hair-raising U-turn on one of the more treacherous canyon roads. I let out a scream as he missed the edge of the cliff by no more than a couple of inches." Amy laughed. "Then he stopped the cab, turned around, and pointed out that I obviously wasn't as intent on calling it quits as I'd thought."

"Almost killing both of you in the process. It's a good thing his brakes were working," the ever-practical Maggie said.

"Hank has a way of making a point." Amy smiled. "But he did save my life as well as help me turn it around. Instead of ending up with a stomach full of sleeping pills that night, I was stuffed with Miss May's fabulous pot roast and boysenberry pie. I've been here ever since. Thanks to Hank hooking me up with Soup, I even pay my way these days. He's one hell of a guy."

Maggie learned a few days later that Hank had also been responsible for Rita's and Hutch's arrivals at Miss May's boardinghouse. It hadn't taken her long to discover that Hutch and Miss May were very much in love with each other, thoroughly immersed in a tender old-fashioned courtship.

Maggie had been helping Miss May polish silver on her third afternoon at the boardinghouse when Miss May told her that she and Hutch had been carrying on their demure love affair for fifteen years.

"We met," Miss May said, "at a tea party, of all

places. An old school friend of mine that I'd known for forty years used to hold an annual reunion for old chums. Poor thing, Emily's in a nursing home now. But she did have wonderful teas back then. Anyway, one of her guests was Laura Roy. You probably don't remember her."

"A silent-screen star, wasn't she?"

Miss May nodded. "She was quite the rage for a while. Even made a few talkies, until she married a successful real estate man and gave up movies for society life. She always arrived at Emily's parties dressed to the hilt. She would hire a chauffeur-driven limo for the occasion, even though rumor had it that her dead husband had left her little more than their fashionable home and a large pile of bills. Timothy drove her that day. He stood by his Bentley all afternoon. I brought him a cup of tea, which quite shocked Laura, who didn't believe in acknowledging the existence of servants. After the party, she very kindly offered to have Timothy drive me home, despite my *faux pas.*"

Miss May chuckled. "After Timothy dropped Laura at her rather crumbling estate off Sunset, we drove around for several hours talking. Oh, Timothy was a bit reticent at first, but after he realized that we shared many interests in common, he opened up. I brought him here for dinner that night. I lived alone then. Didn't start taking in boarders until Henry came along."

"Don't tell me. You met Hank when he was driving his cab."

"He'd just gotten it a week before. He was very

proud of that cab. Mind you, I almost never took taxis—too costly for my budget. But I'd injured my hip in a fall and couldn't face the bus ride to the social security office. I told him a bit about my personal life and a bit about my minor financial difficulties too. Hank had a plan worked out for me before we arrived back here." She laughed louder, a deep, resonant laugh. "Do you know, he moved in the next day? And a few weeks later, he brought Amy along. Then, of course, Rita. Dear Rita. She lost her husband tragically last year when he was in an automobile accident. She was in a terrible state of grief. Why, the day she got into Hank's taxi, she had decided the only answer was for her to go to some small town in New Mexico and live with her daughter, who had only offered to take her in out of obligation."

"This is getting a little unbelievable, Miss May. Do you mean to tell me that Hank finds all your boarders this way?"

Miss May looked thoughtful. "Well, not Timothy, of course. He's been a regular visitor here for fifteen years, after all. But then, if it weren't for Henry, I imagine dear Timothy would still be using up all his meager pension on gasoline to make the daily ride here from his dreary room in Pasadena. I'd been trying to get Timothy to move in here for years, but for all his bravado, Timothy Hutchins is quite old-fashioned. He felt it might compromise me if he moved in."

"I'm surprised," Maggie said, "that he didn't ask you to marry him in all these years."

"Oh, but he did. Many times. I suppose I'm a

stubborn old woman. Too set in my ways. I've had many marriage proposals in my life, but I've just never been the marrying type. I do love Timothy dearly, though. And thanks to Henry convincing him to take up residence here, things have been quite lovely."

Maggie wasn't the least bit surprised that Hank had managed the maneuver. In the few weeks that she had come to know Henry Collier August, she had become thoroughly versed in his manipulative skills. He had succeeded, despite all her objections, in getting her out of the house each day. His cab was still in the body shop, and he seemed content to spend his time dragging her around L.A. showing her the sights, after discovering that although she'd lived in town for over two years, Maggie had seen little of the city beyond the insides of dance studios and movie sets.

Still, Hank August's notion of sightseeing—like everything else about the man—was completely unique. He'd taken her on a tugboat ride off the L.A. docks, on a tour of a nearly unheard-of museum of extinct animals, and to an ongoing dig for Indian artifacts in Orange Grove. He had even rented a bicycle built for two, rigging a strap around Maggie's cast and one of the pedals, and taking her for a Sunday ride through Griffith Park.

Then, most evenings after dinner, Hank would convince her to hobble along with him to Ocean Front Walk in Venice, with its festive carnival atmosphere. They would munch on candy apples, play electronic games in the arcades, take a ride on the carousel at the end of the pier, and watch the sun set over the Pacific.

Maggie had even gotten used to Hank endlessly taking photos of her, although she did find it disconcerting to see blow-ups of herself on the walls of the boardinghouse. Hank might not have wanted to display his talents for money or success, but he thoroughly enjoyed displaying them for sheer pleasure. And as much as Maggie found her physical appearance less than enthralling, she had to admit his photos were superb. She only grew uncomfortable when Hank told her in no uncertain terms that she was spectacular-looking.

Maggie stretched, falling back onto the bed. As she lay there thinking about these past two weeks of carefree days with Hank, she realized that he was slowly casting a spell over her. Instead of continuing to anger and frustrate her, Henry Collier August had managed to delight and amuse her—and, she had to admit, fascinate her. That thought was disturbing, but she told herself that this was merely a brief, pleasant interlude, and as long as her relationship remained friendly and platonic, she was on safe ground.

Maggie closed her eyes, listening to the faint strains of Rita's exercise music as it filtered through the walls. Hank had told her last night that he was planning a special treat for today. She needed something special. Tomorrow morning she was due back at the hospital for X-rays. If they weren't greatly improved from the pictures taken last week, Dr. Fieldston had told her he would have to operate, temporarily inserting a steel pin to see if that would help speed up the healing process. The thought brought terror and panic to Maggie's heart, but she refused to believe her leprechauns would ever fail her so completely..

She quickly sat up, swinging her legs out of bed. Not bothering with the cumbersome crutches, she half-hopped across the room. The bathroom she shared with Amy was two doors down the hall.

When she stepped out of her room, she saw Hank standing by the parlor watching Rita and her group do their aerobic bends and twists. He noticed Maggie and walked over to her.

"Hurry and get dressed. I thought for sure you would never be able to sleep through this racket. Remember, we have a big day today," he said, ruffling her tousled red hair.

"How big?" Maggie asked cautiously. "I have to warn you, I'm in a lousy mood today. My mind keeps wandering to that X-ray machine that's waiting to spell out my fate tomorrow."

"Tomorrow won't come for another day. Why spoil this one?"

Maggie grinned. "I should have known you'd come up with something wise and philosophic. This time, I have to agree with you."

He leaned over and kissed her lightly on the cheek. "See? We're making progress."

Maggie eyed him curiously. Except for that first day at Miss May's when they'd shared that one passionate kiss, Hank had made no further attempts at seduction. Maggie had to admit that there were a few times these past two weeks that she found herself wishing he would try again. But she knew that if he did come on strongly, it would give her a great excuse to back off from a relationship that was growing more and more pleasant. Maybe Hank realized the same thing. "Just what kind of progress are you aiming for?"

"You have a suspicious mind, Maggie Doyle."

"What do you mean?" she asked defensively, further disconcerted by the tender look in his deep brown eyes.

Hank bent low, his lips against her ear. "Only when you want to, Maggie. Only then. I told you when I first met you that I believe in letting things happen naturally."

Maggie backed off, nearly colliding with the door to her bedroom. His sensual words and warm breath sent her pulse racing and made her cheeks burn, but her anger flared up with equal heat. "I thought I made myself clear from the start. If that's what you're waiting for, you're wasting your time." She started to move, but Hank gripped her arm.

"Don't keep running scared, Maggie."

"Scared of you? You're crazy."

Hank reached behind her and turned the doorknob. Maggie would have fallen into her room had Hank not kept a firm grip on her. He half-lifted her inside, closing the door behind him.

"What—what are you doing?" Maggie's voice

quivered, her anger draining abruptly as panic flooded her.

"Sometimes," Hank said softly, his large hands poised on her waist, "it's necessary to illustrate a point." Without another word, he swept Maggie into his arms and kissed her with fierce intensity, his tongue parting her lips and reaching deep into the warmth of her mouth, demanding and getting the passionate response he knew Maggie felt inside. His hands glided up her ribcage until the tips of his fingers caressed her small, firm breasts.

Maggie was trembling. Taken so completely by surprise, she found herself unable to raise her protective wall, unable to do anything but give in to the melting, intoxicating experience of being kissed by such a sensual, tender man.

When he stopped kissing her, Maggie pressed her head against his shoulder, her breathing shallow, her body still shaking. Hank stroked her hair, his own breathing much quicker now.

"I've wanted to do that for the past two weeks," he said softly.

"I don't think I could have handled it." She looked up at him. "I still don't." A small smile creased her lips. "But you did make your point."

Hank ran a finger lightly down her throat. "I enjoyed making it."

Maggie sighed. "Hank, I don't think this is a very good idea."

"It's more than an idea."

"I still think you're crazy. This whole thing is crazy. I'm just biding my time here. Don't you

73

realize that? As soon as this cast comes off, I'm gone. Why complicate matters?"

"They're already complicated, Maggie. Love does that to people."

"Love? Come on, Hank. Let's not get carried away. We hardly know each other. I mean, a couple of kisses—" She stopped short. "Or is this one of your theories about love of humanity or something equally profound? Am I about to make a fool of myself by assuming the wrong interpretation?"

Hank smiled broadly. "No, I wouldn't say it was the wrong interpretation. And I do know a lot about you, Maggie Doyle. I know that you have a terrific laugh, a dramatic temper, a wealth of tender feelings, passion and—"

"And a firm, unyielding dedication to my profession. That comes first. And that seems to have been eliminated from your list."

Hank skimmed her lips with the tip of his finger. "Ah, the taste of success." He gave her a long, intriguing look, making Maggie distinctly uncomfortable.

Looking away, she said, "You may presume you know all about me, but I don't feel that I know anything about you. What makes you tick, Hank? What really happened back in Oregon? What made you give up everything—politics, your family?"

Hank smiled. "Get dressed. Hutch has the Bentley idling outside." He opened the door, the lively music from the parlor mingling with grunts and pants from the ladies. Turning back to

74

Maggie, his brown eyes crinkled up at the edges. "I'm glad you're curious about me. Another sign of progress, don't you agree?"

Maggie shook her head. "Will you get out of here before we have all of Venice thinking something is going on?" She held up her hand as he opened his mouth. "And don't you dare say something *is* going on."

When she was dressed and ready to leave, Hutch tossed Maggie's crutches into the trunk while Hank helped her into the gleaming Bentley. It was a beautiful, clear, early spring day, a rarity in smoggy L.A. The winds must have been blowing just the right way, at least over Venice.

"Where are we going?" Maggie asked, smoothing her white cotton dress as she sank into the cool burgundy leather seat.

"It's March nineteenth," Hank said, as though that explained everything.

"Your birthday?"

He chuckled. "No. That's not for five more months."

"Okay, I give up."

"It's a day for a miracle."

"Well, I could use a miracle," Maggie said wryly, still in the dark about where Hank was taking her.

Hutch got on the freeway heading south, which still gave Maggie no clue as to where they were going. She made a few more attempts to pry their destination out of Hank, but he seemed intent on making it a surprise.

Maggie gave up, settling back into her seat, trying to find a comfortable position for her leg. Hank came to her rescue, lifting her cast carefully and sliding her leg onto his lap. Maggie shot him a guarded look, but Hank only gave her one of his winning smiles.

She *was* more comfortable, she admitted, turning slightly and letting herself relax. In the easy silence, she tilted her head and studied Hank thoughtfully. He met her gaze.

"You're waiting for me to quench your curiosity."

Maggie nodded. "A mind reader, along with all your other enviable skills."

"I was being flip that first day when I told you I was a terrific politician. Actually, I was lousy at it. Funny how a person can be lousy at something and successful at the same time. Well," he said, his deep voice tinged with irony, "not really funny when you consider the strong backing I had from my father-in-law. Gil Hamilton is a very powerful force in Oregon, even though he's been out of office for over eighteen years. He's what you'd call the key man behind the scenes. Very dynamic, charismatic, determined. A man who's rarely thwarted in his efforts to get what he wants."

"Until Henry Collier August came along?"

Hank smiled ruefully at Maggie. "I'm afraid I was his pawn for a long time. Far longer than I like owning up to. I started out as a starry-eyed innocent, full of ideals and great intentions, going back to childhood. I was the kid who always got elected class president. I had these great platforms—extra recess time, no white shirts at assembly, repealing the prohibition against chewing gum. I should have smartened up back then. I never did get the system to go along with any of my demands. But I kept right on trying. My whole family—Mom, Dad, my two younger brothers—were convinced I was destined for great things. I was going to make it to the top. They used to address my mail to President Henry Collier August when I went off to college." He laughed softly for a moment.

"Then along came Lucy Hamilton, ready, willing, and able to help me in my earnest quest for a great future in politics. Lucy and I met in graduate school. I was thrilled to be dating the daughter of a former governor. We were both in political science. Lucy used to talk about running for governor herself one day, but I came to see that she really preferred to fill the same role her father enjoyed playing so much—the power behind the scenes.

"I think from the start both Lucy and Gil saw me as the answer to their prayers. I was earnest, hard-working, and as innocent as the day is long. Lucy and I got married during my last year of graduate school, helped out by Gil's generosity. He used to say it was his way of investing in the future of Oregon"—Hank gave Maggie a wry glance—"as well as his investment in the future of our great country. Gil didn't intend to have me stop at governor. I was slated to go the whole route."

"And the idea didn't grab you?" Maggie asked.

"Oh, it grabbed me for a while. I know this will come as a surprise to you, but I was, once upon a time, a very ambitious fellow. I was the youngest man to win a seat in Oregon's senate. And I had more than a few fantasies about sticking my feet up on my desk in the Oval Office someday."

Maggie looked down at Hank's well-worn sneakers. "I hope you would have bought a decent pair of shoes first," she said, grinning.

"Black ones with pointy tips, just like Gil Hamilton's. Lucy bought me a few pairs from the same shop where her father got his. I wouldn't wear them, so we compromised on cordovan loafers." He lifted his feet. "I have a special fondness for these beat-up things."

"Tell me about you and Lucy. You sound so cynical when you talk about her."

"Do I? I suppose I am cynical now. It's my way of dealing with betrayal."

"Betrayal?"

Hank took a long, slow breath. "I didn't find her locked in the arms of another man or anything like that. Lucy's passion didn't run in that direction. She was faithful in that way. But she wasn't faithful in ways that were just as important to me—maybe even more important."

"I don't understand."

Hank took Maggie's hand, squeezing it gently. "Neither did I, at first." He stroked her arm idly, his eyes drifting to the window, watching the scenery pass by. "I was campaigning for my second term as state senator and had some strong

78

competition. Richard Holmstead was a well-respected lawyer with solid backing, but I was pretty confident I would win. The problem was, by then I wasn't so sure I *wanted* to. I felt like my life was slipping away, that I'd somehow lost control, my sense of what I wanted to achieve. Somewhere along the road to success, I started losing sight of my high ideals. I was supposed to be fighting for the underdog, and there I was living in a fancy estate, replete with cook and housekeeper, driving a classy sports car, hobnobbing with Oregon's leading citizens, being talked into more compromises than I would ever have dreamed possible."

"So one day you woke up and said, the hell with it all?" she asked.

Hank laughed. "You're pretty close. Actually, my blinders suddenly got a rip in them and I saw things painfully clearly one day. You see, my wife and my father-in-law didn't believe in trusting the citizens of the state to elect the right man for the office—namely me, of course. They decided they ought to make sure things worked out the way they wanted."

He looked back out the window. "Remember Watergate?"

"Yes, of course."

"Well, you'd think Gil and Lucy would have learned from that little lesson in history, but as they say, history does have a way of repeating itself. Or it would have, if I hadn't discovered that my wife and father-in-law were engineering a break-in at Holmstead's offices. Once I un-

79

earthed the plot, a lot of other ugly wheeling and dealing floated up to the surface. The public never got wind of it, but I decided to withdraw from the campaign anyway. Lucy said if I did, we were through."

Maggie touched Hank's shoulder. His eyes lifted up to meet hers. "Not an easy decision," she said softly, feeling a sudden urge to put her arms around him. But she did nothing more than let her hand slide down to his.

"I couldn't play the game anymore, not once I saw what the rules were really all about. Lucy wanted me to be someone I never was or could be. So now I make up my own rules, and I go to bed at night feeling like—well, like a human being. It's a great feeling."

"What about your children? You left them as well as your wife."

"I actually see them more now than I did when I was living in Oregon. I was so busy being a politician then that I had no time or energy left over for being a father. Since I've been here, they spend all their vacations with me, summers, lots of holidays. Joanie is eleven, very bright, sassy, and outgoing. Michael is nine. He's serious, astute, and tender. He loves animals. Wants to be a vet when he grows up. We have wonderful times together. Quality time. It took awhile for all of us to adjust. It's hard explaining to your friends at school that your father, a state senator, dropped out to become a cab driver in Venice, California. Especially when their mother thinks it's the crime of the century."

Maggie saw a flash of pain crease Hank's brow. She wondered, for all his feeling betrayed by his wife, if he still didn't love her. She found the thought disturbing, which didn't in any way mesh with her plan to stay uninvolved. Yet the more she learned about Hank, the closer she felt to him.

Suddenly, Hank swept his arms around her, his mood shifting dramatically. "Okay, get ready for a miracle," he said brightly as Hutch brought the Bentley to a halt.

Maggie looked out the window. Throngs of people were gathered just ahead, milling about a wide piazza, standing around a gushing fountain and an old Spanish mission. Overhead and sweeping onto the stone walk and the semitropical greenery were hundreds of birds, their iridescent green plumage shimmering like emeralds in the bright sunlight.

It was March nineteenth, St. Joseph's Day, and like clockwork the swallows had come back to Capistrano. Maggie smiled, delighted by the scene, as Hank helped her out of the car. He bought them both some birdseed. Hutch was invited to join them, but he decided to drive back to Venice, suggesting that Hank call when he wanted to be picked up.

As a few bold swallows whizzed close to Maggie's shimmering red hair, she pressed against Hank. Then, acting purely on impulse and desire, she swept her arms around him, kissing him full on the mouth and sending his birdseed plummeting to the ground. The swallows danced around them as they embraced. Hank looked down at Maggie and grinned broadly. Maybe more than one miracle happened on March nineteenth.

CHAPTER FIVE

Hank knew that his favorite picture of Maggie would be the one he took as she stood at the fountain. Chirping birds fluttered overhead, the misty water sprayed her face, and a gentle breeze blew her luxuriant red hair so that it looked like sparks of fire. A swallow alit and perched for a moment on the palm of her hand nibbling birdseed, just as Hank got the shot. More than anything, it was the look on Maggie's face that enthralled him: enchantingly vibrant, filled with delight, and, if only for now, free of tension and fear.

"Let's go have a drink at the café across the street," Maggie suggested when she'd used up her fourth bag of birdseed. "And some food. I'm starving." She started to bend down to retrieve her crutches, but Hank slipped one arm around her waist.

"Okay, my tender swallow, open your mouth," he teased, trickling some birdseed over her hair. Then, moving very close, he brushed off the strands.

Maggie noticed for the first time that Hank

had a hint of a cleft on his chin. She touched her finger to the spot. "Nice," she whispered, letting him slip her finger up to his lips, letting herself feel happy, sexy, and a touch provocative amidst the safety of the crowd.

There were many lovers in San Juan Capistrano that day. Those who noticed Maggie and Hank standing with their arms around each other, kissing tenderly in the center of the broad piazza, smiled; more than a few couples followed their lead.

When Hank stopped kissing Maggie, he continued to hold on to her. "Let's stay just like this until the birds fly south."

"And when is that?"

"October twenty-third."

"You're sure?"

"They're very punctual."

Maggie gave him a light kiss on the faint cleft in his chin. Then she looked up into his large brown eyes. "I'm afraid I can't make it to October. How about if we—stay until tomorrow instead?"

Maggie could feel her heart begin to pound faster and faster as Hank traced a fine line with his fingers across her cheek and down her slender neck. It was an intimate, tender gesture, all the response she needed.

Hank bent down and lifted her crutches. As Maggie took them from him, she felt a flash of panic. This wasn't the way she'd planned to cope with her escalating attraction toward Hank August. She was going to play it cool, keep everything under control, and leave with no regrets. But something more powerful than her common sense had taken possession of her. She had never felt such stinging desire before, the kind of desire that, without warning, swooped down like the graceful swallows, filled with similar purpose, determination, and hunger. All at once, she broke out into laughter.

"What's so funny?" Hank asked, amused and relieved to see that the momentary panic he could read so easily in her expression had passed.

"Oh, I was just thinking," she said, as they made their way through the crowd, "about that first day in your cab when you told me that you believed in feeding the senses."

"Starving senses," Hank grinned. "I've written an essay on the subject, giving you due credit for coining such an intriguing phrase."

Maggie stopped for a second and looked at him. "It suddenly hit me how undernourished some of my senses have become."

Hank smiled, a very sensual, enticing smile. "Let me take care of that."

They went across the street to the café, which was part of a small hotel that faced the ruined stone mission that had been destroyed over a hundred and fifty years ago in an earthquake. While Maggie ordered a late lunch for the two of them, Hank went inside to see about a room. Fortunately, although the hotel had been booked solid last night with tourists who wanted to be on hand for the day of the miracle, many were checking out this afternoon. Hank was able to get a terraced room overlooking the piazza. As he signed the register, he realized that his hands were trembling.

Out of practice, he told himself, knowing, even as he had the thought, that it was more than that. For three years he'd led a carefree, contented life, free of the kind of duties, responsibilities, and involvements that might in any way suck him slowly back into the life-style that he wanted to avoid at all costs. Except for his children and the residents of Miss May's boardinghouse, Hank had not gotten close to very many people. And his sexual relationships since Lucy had all been casual and unencumbered. He had told himself, as he'd told Maggie that day in his cab, that he was open to love if it happened along. Now he wasn't so sure.

Maggie had awakened something inside him that he had begun to doubt existed. She made his pulse race, his palms sweat, his heart pound loudly in his chest. She captured his dreams at night and his thoughts during the day. She had made him see that, for all his contentment, something had been missing in his life. And seeing that, he knew that when she left he would feel a void he'd never felt before.

He walked outside, standing at the entry for a minute to watch Maggie, her face tilted up to the sun, a spattering of freckles across the bridge of her nose, long thick lashes shadowing fine cheekbones, a tiny smile curving her full, sensual lips. Hank could still feel his hands trembling, but looking at Maggie now, he knew it was pure desire that engulfed him.

"What did you order for us?" he asked, his voice a touch husky as he told himself patience was a virtue. In truth, he would have gladly skipped lunch, wanting only to feast on Maggie.

Maggie's eyes held an aura of bewitchment. "I told the waiter to bring us the quickest thing on the menu."

"A perfect choice." He grinned, reaching across the table for her hand.

Within a couple of minutes, two chef salads arrived, along with a carafe of wine. They both ate quickly, leaving half the food on their plates, managing less than a glass each of the chilled Chablis.

Hank brought the two wineglasses and the carafe to their room on the second floor. Maggie was slightly breathless from the climb, having refused to let Hank carry her up the stairs.

"I want to do this on my own two feet, such as they are," she'd said, that determined expression that he found so captivating lighting up her face.

In their room, Maggie opened the French windows and stepped out onto the terrace. Hank brought out a glass of wine for each of them.

"It really is a magical day," she whispered, leaning against him as he set her crutches against the balustrade and handed her a goblet.

He smoothed her thick, tousled hair and then tapped her glass with his. "To miracles. May they never cease."

Maggie smiled, taking a small sip of wine. Then

she looked up into Hank's eyes. "I've never made love with a cast on," she said, her expression suddenly shy.

Hank skimmed her lips with the tip of his tongue, his hands reaching around her. "I promise I won't tickle the toes on that foot." Then he lifted her up in his arms, this time with no protest, and carried Maggie back inside the room. He set her down on her good foot on the thick cranberry carpet.

As Hank slowly slid down the zipper on Maggie's dress, she felt herself tighten, but as his cool fingers lightly, tenderly caressed the silky skin of her back, her muscles relaxed. She reached out and with tremulous hands began unbuttoning his shirt. Opening it fully, she ran her hands over his broad, muscular chest. Hank felt a shiver ripple through him at her touch.

They kissed then with hunger and passion that only fanned their desire. Hank slipped the dress down over Maggie's shoulders, and she shrugged it off, letting it fall in a heap to the floor. Then he peeled away her lacy undergarments and stepped back a few inches to take in her slender yet strong body, the body of a dancer, firm, elegant, graceful. He lifted her in his arms again and carried her over to the bed.

Maggie made an effort to pull him down with her, his steady gaze making her shy again, but Hank merely knelt beside her.

"You're incredibly beautiful, Maggie." As he spoke, his hands glided over her breasts, his palms skimmed her taut nipples, moving down over her well-defined ribcage; his fingers then spread around her small waist, and finally slid down to her narrow hips.

Maggie felt her body tremble, and her breathing was uneven. Her lips parted slightly, and Hank, who hadn't wanted to stop memorizing every curve and line of her exquisite body, couldn't resist pulling her to him for a deep, passionate kiss. Then they fell back onto the pillows.

Hank arched his back, slipping off his trousers and briefs. Then he knocked off his sneakers, shoved them from the edge of the bed with his heel, and turned onto his side to face Maggie.

With a pleasure quite new to her—sex in the past had not been a frequent occurrence and had never once been filled with the kind of intense, fiery need she was now experiencing—Maggie boldly studied him, her large green eyes moving slowly from his sensuous mouth to his firm, muscular legs. Her trembling hands stroked down to his belly, Hank's body shivering with a sharp bolt of desire. As her fingers tantalizingly caressed the inside of his thighs, he moaned with pleasure, his own hands stroking her buttocks, then slipping intimately between her legs.

Maggie shivered, pressing more tightly against him, her hands winding around his waist. "I've never felt this way before." She gasped as he forcefully tugged her higher so that his lips could encircle first one rigid nipple, then the other, his tongue flickering across them so that Maggie began to writhe in exquisite agony, the rest of her words catching in her throat.

89

"Oh, Maggie, this is the way it should be for us," Hank murmured, his hands cupping her face as he moved on top of her, careful of the cast Maggie had all but forgotten.

She smiled tremulously at him, then barely mouthed the words, "Don't stop now."

Her good leg swung around the back of his thighs as she experienced the intoxicating relief of his entry. It was as though her whole being had been poised for this moment. Their breath exploded in short sporadic gasps as they moved together, passion spiraling with whirlwind speed to an ecstasy that captured them both.

Afterward, he kissed her in a slow, languorous fashion, not trying to hide the joy of possession he was feeling. A tender, amused half-smile played across his lips.

"What are you thinking?" Maggie asked, her hands idly tracing a line from his neck across his broad shoulders.

"That I'd like to photograph you now. You have a delicious look of satisfaction on your face."

"I do?"

"Mmm." He curled a strand of her fiery hair around his finger, then tugged it and forced her lips to his, kissing her lustily.

Released, Maggie fell breathlessly back onto the pillows. "You're right. I must look satisfied. I feel incredibly good." She sighed deeply, then turned onto her side and gently glided her fingers through his thick, dark brown hair. "I'm glad," she said with a funny little smile, "that you

90

didn't marry that lady who was about to be deported."

Hank laughed. "So am I."

"I'm surprised she didn't end up boarding at Miss May's. From what I hear, you bring all your troubled passengers to her door. Me included." A subtle frown marred her perfect smile. "We're quite a crew, aren't we? Lost souls in a storm. And there you are, holding out a large umbrella, ready to rescue us."

"What's wrong with that?"

Maggie gave him a tender kiss. "You're very special, Hank. Very rare."

"But?"

Maggie's smile broadened, her fingers remaining entwined in his hair. "I could never manage the kind of life you lead. I suppose I'm too selfish, too determined to make it in this competitive world that doesn't seem to touch your spirit."

Hank studied her thoughtfully. "What made you choose choreography rather than becoming a dancer? I can picture you floating like an eloquent vision across a stage, capturing everyone's hearts, being showered with applause and bouquets of red roses to match your hair."

Maggie shrugged. "That isn't me. For one thing, I've always suffered from a terrible case of stage fright. For all my years of recitals and performances, I could never fully let go of my self-consciousness. Besides"—she grinned—"I'm very bossy, a tyrant for perfection. When I was still a teen-ager back in Peoria, my dance instructor, Madame Swindlan, used to be driven crazy

91

by my need to alter steps and movement sequences. She'd rant and rage, I'd argue back, and we'd both go home with sore throats. Finally, to the relief of all the students who'd grown weary of our shouting matches, she relented and let me choreograph some of the recital segments. At eighteen, feeling very grown-up and desperate to get to where things were happening, I left home and headed for New York."

Maggie sighed. "It took me close to a year to finally get a job with Tina Isaacs's Modern Dance Troupe, then two years of fighting butterflies in my stomach through every performance, before finally convincing Tina, who choreographed every number, to let me apprentice with her.

"It was Tina who introduced me to Chet Castle, probably the best film choreographer in Hollywood. They had a brief but heated affair, long enough, fortunately, for me to get a chance to dazzle him with my talent. By then, Tina was letting me choreograph several dance numbers. I got some good press, and Chet was taken with my energy. So I packed up my bag and shuffled happily off to Hollywood. Rock-style musicals were coming into vogue, and Chet and I barely got a chance to take a deep breath between films. And then the famous Dennis Arcaine flashed into my life for one brief, sparkling moment." Maggie closed her eyes and rolled over onto her back.

Hank stroked her cheek, then tucked his arm under her, drawing her close again. "Is that all you ever wanted, Maggie?"

"When I was growing up, I was one of those

really gawky, shy kids. My mother, a delicate, graceful woman who lived with bitterness about my father never making anything out of his life, found me lacking as well. I guess she took her disappointment out on both of us. Not that she was ever openly cruel. She simply ignored us most of the time. My father found acceptance and escape down at the local pub. Until my mother decided to enroll me in ballet in an effort to combat my utter lack of grace, I spent most of my time alone in my room daydreaming."

Maggie grinned. "I really was dreadful at first —two left feet. Madame nearly tore her silver hair out in frustration. But, thank God, she saw some hope in me. Maybe it was just that I worked so hard. The truth was, I never wanted to go home. After a while, it was just accepted that half my waking hours would be spent at the ballet school. It became everything to me. I treated my ability as a precious gift that rescued me from endless boredom and loneliness, that gave my life meaning. It didn't matter that I dressed abominably, never had a single date in high school, never even knew how to talk to a boy, much less flirt with him. I had talent, ambition, and a driving need to be successful."

"I imagine you will be," Hank said quietly. "I just wonder if it will be more fulfilling for you than it was for me."

"It's different for me, Hank. For one thing I've always avoided intimate relationships. I never had to deal with the tangle of emotions, the complications, the mixed feelings that you had to cope with trying to be a politician, a husband, and a father all at the same time."

Hank rested his chin on his hand, his elbow pressing into the pillow. "Tell me if I'm wrong, but I think we just experienced one of those intimate involvements you always avoid."

Maggie bit down on her lower lip. "You're not wrong." Her eyes shot up to his. "And I'm not going to lie and say I regret my slip into temptation. I've never felt this good before."

"Not even choreographing a perfect number?"

Maggie gave him a shrewd smile. "This is different." The smile faded. "It's also temporary. The two of us—well, it would never work. I'd drive you crazy after a while. I couldn't stand to watch you waste all your talents, just drift through life. I'm much too driven myself. I can't stay in one place. I can't stand the thought of not being the best. I couldn't shift gears at this point. I don't know that I'll ever be able to."

Hank turned her head to face him. "That day I saw you sitting in the back of my cab, acting so cool and unattainable, I thought to myself, what a pity. Here's a woman just aching to drop her guard, let herself go, and she doesn't even know it."

"Oh, Hank, no theorizing, please. Next thing, you'll be telling me my real drive is to make my mother proud of me. Well, she's been dead for seven years, so I'd be wasting my time. I'm not doing this for her. I'm fulfilling a need within me. Let's just enjoy each other while I'm here. Isn't that what you've been preaching? Taking each moment as it comes?"

Hank kissed her lightly. "That was before I fell hopelessly in love."

"Don't." Her expression was a mixture of discomfort and sadness.

"I'm only telling you the truth, Maggie. I think I fell in love with you when I turned around in the cab to snap that picture of you laughing. Of course, it wasn't deep, unabiding love at that point," he said, his eyes sparkling. "That didn't come until you threatened to bash me over the head with my camera."

Maggie laughed. "I should have bopped you. You deserved it." Her laughter faded abruptly. "I should also never have told you to get off the freeway. Then none of this would have happened. You've complicated my life, Hank August."

Hank stretched, then tugged her on top of him. "This is one complication I wouldn't have wanted to miss for anything, not even the thought that it might end."

"Not *might*, Hank. It *is* going to end. It has to."

Hank slid his tongue seductively around the ridge of her earlobe. "We'll take each moment as it comes."

Maggie shook her head. "No, Hank, we have to—"

But then his mouth captured hers, silencing her protest. A few moments later, Maggie forgot the argument completely, too excited to think with any clarity at all.

It was late in the night when Maggie moaned in her sleep, waking herself up. Hank immediately reached out for her.

"What's wrong, Maggie?"

She shivered. "A bad dream."

Hank sat up and wrapped his arms around her slender body. "Talk to me."

She leaned against his shoulder. "I know what those X-rays are going to show tomorrow. I knew it when I saw the doctor's face last time. He was fairly certain then that I'd need the surgery. I think he just couldn't bear to tell me. Maybe he was hoping for some kind of miracle."

"Miracles do happen," he said softly.

Maggie lifted her head. "Not this time."

They ended up staying awake the rest of the night. At dawn, they were sitting out on the terrace, watching the sun light up the sky as the swallows started chirping. Maggie took in the sight, feeling none of the joy and excitement of yesterday. Hank called Hutch after breakfast, and they barely spoke a word as they waited for him to arrive.

Maggie was drifting off, floating over misty mountains, twirling as a breeze caught hold of her billowing skirt. And then she was an emerald-plumed swallow, swooping over the ruined stone church, around and around, faster and faster—

"Maggie?"

She opened her eyes, blinking several times to

96

adjust to the soft light. She felt dizzy and light-headed, unsure of where she was. And then she remembered. "How did it go?"

Hank placed a cool hand on her moist cheek. She'd been crying in her half-conscious state. "It went very well. And they were able to give you a cast you can walk on this time—in a couple of days."

Maggie stared bleakly at him. "Terrific."

She closed her eyes and drifted off again. Hank sat at her bedside, watching large teardrops roll silently down her cheeks again as she sailed off amidst the haze of soft, whirring hospital sounds.

He was exhausted. It was four in the morning. He'd stayed with Maggie from the time they'd arrived that afternoon to have her X-rays taken and then meet with Fieldston, who had already called in a specialist to act as consultant. Maggie had been right, her sixth sense working only too well. The X-rays confirmed something Fieldston had strongly suspected all week: The shattered bone refused to mesh properly, and the only hope at this point, if Maggie was to continue her strenuous career, was to opt for surgery. Milton Owens, chief of orthopedics, seconded Fieldston's opinion.

There was nothing for Maggie to do but sullenly nod her head in agreement. Her only wish was to get it over with as quickly as possible. A minor miracle, but not one to put the least sparkle in Maggie's eyes, was that Fieldston was able to arrange for the surgery that evening.

Despite Hank's continuing support and encouragement, Maggie grew petulant and agitated as the time for the operation approached. She kept telling Hank to leave, but he refused. Then, at the last minute, just before the nurse stuck a hypodermic needle filled with a fast-acting sedative into her arm, Maggie suddenly grabbed for Hank, clinging to him. When he pressed his lips lightly to hers, she responded with frantic urgency, which made the gray-haired nurse flush. Maggie and Hank remained oblivious to her discomfort as he continued to hold her fiercely against him, whispering soothing words, stroking her back. Finally, the nurse cleared her throat, saying that she really had to get Maggie ready for the surgery.

Hank kissed her one more time, feeling Maggie pull back into her shell with stoic resolve. He stepped aside, and the nurse jabbed her arm. She was already drifting off as the orderlies wheeled her out of the room. Hank followed, holding her limp hand until he was told he could go no further. With reluctance, he pressed her hand to his lips and then placed it gently by her side. Maggie made a vague attempt at a smile.

When Maggie awoke for the second time, it was seven in the morning and the nurse had brought in her breakfast. Hank was slumped in an uncomfortable green plastic chair, sound asleep. The nurse shook him gently and then left the room. He was wide awake instantly; his eyes immediately moved to Maggie.

"You better go home and get some decent sleep. You look awful," Maggie said.

He got up to stretch his stiff limbs, then sat down on the edge of her bed. He studied her carefully. He didn't like what he saw: the grim set of her green eyes, the defeated line about her mouth, her resigned voice devoid of expression. She turned her head away.

"Dr. Fieldston was very optimistic, Maggie. There's no reason to feel so down."

"I'm tired, Hank. Just go, okay?"

"Not with you feeling like this," he said stubbornly. "I want to know what's whirling around in that head of yours."

"Dammit!" She glared at him hotly. "Just because we spent one afternoon in bed doesn't give you special claim to my private thoughts. I'm sorry it ever happened. I'm sorry I ever stepped into that damn cab of yours." She took a long, deep breath. "And I just don't feel like playing the nice, sweet, cheerful patient this moment." She refused to meet his steady gaze. "Would you ask the nurse to come in on your way out?"

Hank shook his head. "Okay. I'll let you lie here and wallow in self-pity for a few hours. I'm too tired to argue with you or prove that you don't mean what you're saying." He cupped her chin, forcing her to face him. "Look, I still have a bruised lip from that kiss you gave me before you went under last night." He puckered out his lower lip, his eyes sparkling despite her sullen glare. "Don't worry, I'll let you make it all better later on."

"Damn you, Hank. Don't you ever accept defeat?"

"Only when the final vote has been cast. And then there's always recount." He got up and started for the door. "I wrote a great essay on the essence of defeat a few months ago," he said, turning back to her. "I was inspired by this battered boxer I picked up one night in my cab. He'd just landed flat on his butt for the twenty-fourth time out of twenty-seven fights. He sat there nursing a swollen eye and bruised ribs while he gave me a blow-by-blow account of the fight. I asked him why the hell he kept stepping into the ring with that kind of a record." Hank paused, a teasing smile on his face.

"Well," Maggie gave in, "what did he say?"

"He told me that he had nothing better to do on a Friday night, and as long as he could still climb out of the ring after the fight, he figured he wasn't doing so bad."

"You *would* find his philosophy inspirational," she said sarcastically.

Hank ignored her cutting remark. "When the next Friday rolled around, I took Miss May and Oscar and went to see him fight. Guess what happened?"

"He landed flat on his butt."

"Right." He winked. "But his next time out, he won the fight in the first round. So when you're through feeling defeated and you're ready to get off your butt, I'll come fight a few rounds with you."

He walked out then, rubbing his lower lip and leaving her lying in bed, furious. But at least she'd lost that bleak, sullen look.

CHAPTER SIX

Maggie had been back at Miss May's for four days. Her walking cast, made of lightweight waterproof plastic, reached from her foot up to her midcalf and provided her with a lot more mobility. But since returning from the hospital, Maggie had barely left her room. No matter how much she argued with herself, she seemed unable to muster the energy to get out, unable to shake the sense of doom engulfing her.

This was just the way it had gone for that dancer in Tina Isaacs's troupe. First the cast, then one operation after another, until the decision was finally reached to fuse the bone together as the only recourse. Which meant the loss of flexibility and the end of a career.

Not that there weren't choreographers who had certain physical handicaps. But they had made their name first, established themselves. Maggie was just starting out in the business—and a dog-eat-dog business at that. Nobody out there was ready to do her any favors.

Maggie knew that everyone at Miss May's—including Miss May herself—was worried about her. They had tried reasoning with her, cajoling her, enticing her, arguing with her. No one had made any headway. Maggie had withdrawn from the nest, locking herself away both physically and emotionally.

As for Hank, his cab had finally come out of the body shop and he was back at work. He stopped by her door each night, but she refused to answer him. He seemed the least disturbed of anyone about her reclusive behavior, which, Maggie told herself, was a relief—except that it got to her. In fact, it quite infuriated her to think that he regarded her withdrawal so casually. She used his seemingly cool disinterest in her misery as an excuse to silently berate him for being insincere, unfeeling, self-involved. And then she turned on herself, furious for having let Hank literally sweep her off her feet that day in San Juan Capistrano. She conveniently forgot that she was the one who'd made the first move.

On Friday morning, Maggie woke up to the sound of shrieking children. Rita's day-care group had arrived. Maggie rolled over and turned on her radio, trying to drown out the sound. She usually liked hearing the noise of their laughter, the tiny voices filled with energy and excitement. Last week, she'd even gone in and read a few stories to the children, much to Rita's delight. Hutch had been there that day, too. Three children had gathered around him as he showed them how to erect a large, towerlike structure out of wooden blocks. Throughout the morning, Miss May bustled in and out with

102

homemade cookies, juice, and funny old clothes for dress-up. Maggie, who had rarely spent any time with children, found that she thoroughly enjoyed herself.

This morning, the joyful shrieks depressed her. She rolled over and pulled the covers up around her ears. There was a knock on her door.

"Yes?" she answered only after the rapping kept up.

"It's me. Rita. The children would love to have you read to them again, Maggie. How about it?"

"Not today."

"Oh, come on. You had such a good time last week. Don't let them down."

"No, really. Another time. I'm kind of tired this morning. And—I have a splitting headache."

"Well, they'll be here until eleven thirty. You rest, and I'll check with you a bit later."

Maggie sighed. Well, at least she was off the hook for the moment. Another knock on her door proved her wrong.

"I have some breakfast for you, Maggie." Miss May's deep voice had a no-nonsense sound about it.

Maggie knew it would do no good to tell her she wasn't hungry. Miss May would insist, as she had each day before, that she absolutely must eat three healthy meals a day, and she would tolerate nothing less.

Maggie moved sluggishly out of bed, walked across the room, and opened the door. Miss May, carrying a silver tray laden with eggs, cereal, juice, and coffee, marched in and set the food on a table by the window.

"My Lord, child, you look peaked. When did you comb your hair last? It looks like a robin's nest. Come here and sit down."

Maggie did as she was ordered, and Miss May, gently but firmly, began brushing Maggie's thick, tangled locks.

"You do that very well," Maggie said, letting her eyes close, her muscles relaxing a little for the first time in over a week.

"I must spend hours each week doing this for the children at the Institute."

"The Institute? Oh, yes. Oscar's—home. Hank told me you do volunteer work there."

Miss May set the brush down and moved around to face Maggie. "As a matter of fact, I'm off to Santa Lucia this morning. Why don't you come with me? Oscar asks about you every time I see him. He'd be so happy if you came to visit. It would be such a relief for him to know you're doing better. When you didn't come down for dinner the other night when he was over, he sat in a corner all evening not talking to anyone. Wouldn't even play his flute."

"I don't think I could handle it, Miss May. Not today. Maybe another time."

Miss May shook her head wearily. "I believe those were your exact words to Rita. Don't you see that you're throwing your days away, Maggie? You have so much to offer, and you sit here cheating yourself and others of your gifts. I know you told me your career means everything to you, but I believe you've never given yourself a chance to see that there are many other wonderful things that you're capable of giving and receiving."

"Miss May, I don't mean to be rude. You've certainly been kinder and more caring toward me than almost anyone I've ever known. I know what you're trying to do, but—I just need to go through this in my own way. Please understand."

"Well, at least get dressed and join us for lunch at noon. And then maybe some fresh air to put a bit of color back in your cheeks."

Maggie smiled, saying nothing, remaining noncommittal. When Miss May left, she locked her door, praying no one else would come by for a while. She ignored the breakfast Miss May had worked so hard on and climbed back into bed. Later, she would have to remember to sneak out and flush the food down the toilet, or Miss May would have a fit.

Although she'd made a strong vow before going to sleep last night to do a few exercises today in an effort to get back into shape—her body looked to her like little more than skin and bone from utter lack of use—Maggie could not work up any enthusiasm for the task. So she told herself "tomorrow" and picked up a magazine until she was tired enough to drift into a morning nap.

Miss May, Hutch, Rita, and Amy were gathered in the dining room eating lunch when Hank arrived home a few minutes after twelve. He scanned the room quickly. Miss May shook her head.

Hank nodded and strode down the hall. He was, he told himself, a remarkably patient man, an understanding, sympathetic man. He was calm, cool, collected. He let very little ruffle his feathers. But he'd had just about enough. There was only so much a man could take.

He rapped loudly on Maggie's door, his face set with grim determination.

"Maggie, open this door."

Maggie sat up abruptly in bed at the sharp tone of Hank's voice. "I'm resting," she said coolly.

"You've had enough rest to last a lifetime. Open the door."

"No. I don't want to talk with you right now."

"Fine. We won't talk. Open it."

"Hank, please go away. I have a right to be alone if I choose to."

"Maggie, I'll give you one more chance. Otherwise, I'm breaking the door down."

"Miss May will kill you," Maggie warned.

"Miss May," Hank shouted, "I'm going to break Maggie's door down. I'll fix it for you later."

Miss May smiled. "That's fine, dear. It sticks anyway," she called out.

The others around the dining table grinned, although they were all a little disconcerted by Hank's manner. He was always so easygoing and rarely raised his voice. But Miss May wasn't the least bit surprised. She knew it only took the right woman to spark a man like Henry Collier August into action. Fire and water. Ah yes, she thought gleefully, a perfect match. She heard the

106

door shatter. There would definitely be some steam now.

"How dare you?" Maggie shrieked. "I can't believe you did that. You have no right—Hank, stay away from me. I'll scream. I warn you, I'll throw this lamp at you."

But Hank reached her before she reached the lamp. He grabbed her arm.

"Okay, out of bed," he demanded, throwing off her covers.

Maggie wrestled free, gripping the edge of the blanket and pulling it back up over her. Meanwhile, Hank was at her bureau, searching through her drawers.

Maggie was incensed. "Get away from my things. I've had just about enough."

"No, *I've* had just about enough," he said, turning and tossing a leotard and tights at her.

"What are those for?"

"Put them on," he ordered. "You're getting off your butt whether you like it or not. Choreographers work out, correct? They have to stay in shape, don't they? Look at you. You're going to hell."

"I will not put those things on. I don't want to get into shape. What for? My next operation?"

"If it turns out that way, yes. Now hurry up. By the time your dance group shows up on Monday you'll have to work out all your charley horses."

"What dance group?"

"The one I'm going to tell Rita to organize."

"Oh, no. No way. Listen to me, Henry Collier Au—"

"Sorry. I'm through listening. Get dressed."

Her eyes narrowed. "No."

"Fine. I'll help you."

"You stay away from me!" She backed up against the headboard, on her knees now, gripping the covers around her. Hank strode across the room.

Maggie screamed. "Miss May, Hutch—somebody, dammit—get this maniac out of here!"

In the dining room everyone sat still, all eyes on Miss May. She smiled benignly at each of them. "Do eat your casserole before it gets cold. I'm sure Henry has things under control."

"Miss May!" Maggie screamed louder this time. There was no response. It was beginning to dawn on her that no one had any intention of coming to her rescue.

Hank yanked the covers off. "Last chance."

Maggie glared at him. "I will never speak to you again, Hank August. If you lay one hand on me, I swear I'll walk out of here and you'll never see me again."

She shrieked as he began tugging her nightgown up. Demoralized, she said finally, "All right, dammit. I'll get dressed. But not in that. I'll —I'll put on a dress."

But Hank was not to be dissuaded at this point. He held the tights and leotard out to her. "You can't work out in a dress."

"Oh, please, Hank," she entreated now, drained of rage. "I'm not ready."

He took hold of her shoulders. "If you don't want me to bend your ear with my discourse on

108

postoperative blues, you better hurry up. I could really go on about this one for hours."

"Okay," she relented. "But get out of here first."

"Sorry, I'm not budging."

"This is humiliating," she said, her fury sparked again. "I will not get undressed in front of you."

"I've seen you naked before."

"That was different. And," she added icily, "it was the first and last time."

"And this," he said calmly, "will be the second time. Now, do I get your cooperation, or do I put these things on you myself?"

Maggie, flushed with rage and embarrassment, stormed into her narrow closet, shut the door, and squirmed into her exercise clothes. She stepped back out, perspiring and still furious. "In case you've forgotten, I happen to have a broken ankle. I don't even think I should be exercising."

"I already checked with Fieldston. He thought it was a great idea for you to work out as long as you didn't put any strain on that one foot. I'm sure someone with your great expertise knows enough exercises that won't involve your busted ankle. Shall we go?"

"Where?" she asked cautiously.

"I fixed up a place for you in my spare room, the one my kids stay in when they visit. I'll even let you borrow some of my weights. Later, we'll rent a boat down at the dock and you can row me through the canals of Venice. It's great for the upper torso." He slipped his hand around her waist, but Maggie gave him a searing glance.

"Forget it. This isn't Capistrano," she said tightly, with more determination than she felt. Hank's touch had not lost its effect. She cursed silently as she followed Hank's lingering gaze on her breasts. Through the thin material of the green leotard, her taut nipples left no doubt that he could still arouse her.

She crossed her arms in front of her chest. "Why can't you just leave me alone?"

"To tell you the truth, I don't know. You've manged to completely disrupt my nice, easy-going life. I even forgot to take my camera with me today. Thanks to you, I missed some fantastic shots. Which reminds me," he said cheerily. "Wait till you see the ones I took of you in Capistrano. I have them up in my room."

"I don't want to see your etchings," Maggie said sarcastically.

Hank grinned, his large brown eyes seductive as he scanned her body. "I still wish I'd taken some shots of you in our hotel room."

Maggie reddened and hated herself for it. Damn my Irish complexion, she thought. Her pale coloring made even the slightest blush apparent. To end the conversation and to avoid Hank's provocative smile, she strode across the room.

The cast gave her a funny kind of wiggle, and Hank smiled as he watched her storm over to the door. But he was careful to banish the smile when he came up to her as she struggled with the broken door.

To get to Hank's rooms on the third floor required walking by the parlor and dining room. Before her mishap, Maggie used to think of her leotard as a second skin, more comfortable than any outfit she had. But now she felt almost naked and exposed. She dreaded passing everyone on her way to the stairs. Especially since they must all have heard her entire screaming match with Hank. She hesitated and looked back at Hank.

"There's a back staircase, if you'd rather," he said, tenderness returning to his tone.

As angry as she still was at him, she gave him a grateful nod. He led her around past the empty kitchen and through a rear hall to a steep, narrow staircase that was rarely used.

"This climb alone should count as my exercise for the day," Maggie grumbled as she started up.

Hank came up behind her, swatting her lightly on her rear end. "No chance, sweetheart. I've allotted us forty-five minutes for the first day. I'll follow your lead, of course. You are the professional."

"Us?" She stopped abruptly on the second floor landing.

"I always did want to take private dance lessons. All the football players do ballet or something like that. I figure, once we're limbered up you can teach me some nifty two-steps—nothing too complicated, unless it turns out I have a flair for it. But I'm not rushing you. I've got plenty of time."

A tiny spark lit Maggie's green eyes. So he wanted to work out with her, learn a few dance steps? Well, she thought, feeling a sense of purpose for the first time in weeks, she just might be able to pay Hank August back for humiliating her after all. When she got through with her exercise and dance program, he'd be lucky if he could walk, much less do some "nifty two-steps."

Maggie had a flash of misgiving about her plan when she walked into Hank's spare room. He really had gone all out to set the place up for her, even putting a wide full-length mirror with an exercise barre across one wall and a large professional floor mat on top of the brown carpet.

Trying not to reveal how touched she was, she asked, "When did you do all this?"

Hank stood beside her. "I started it when you were in the hospital. I thought you might feel better given the right atmosphere to work in."

Maggie moved to the full-length mirror, flinching as she stared at herself. She must have dropped at least ten pounds since she'd broken her ankle, ten more pounds than she could afford to lose. And it was amazing, she thought ruefully, what damage a few weeks of inactivity could wreak on muscles; all their firm tautness seemed to have vanished.

Hank came up behind her and unzipped his trousers, much to Maggie's alarm. But as she stepped away defensively she saw that he had a pair of running shorts on. He'd arrived at her room prepared to get his way. He slowly unbuttoned his shirt, his eyes continuing to rest on her.

Maggie knew he was being intentionally provocative. Although she tried her best to stare him down, she finally turned away, finding that his actions prodded too many sensual memories—memories that, much to her despair, she'd had no luck dispelling, for all her concerted efforts to put them out of her mind.

She turned back to the mirror, Hank following suit. In an unconscious gesture, she ran her fingers over her ribcage.

"I told you you'd gone to hell," he teased. "Now, let's get to work. And tonight I'm taking you out for a big pasta dinner so you can start putting some meat back on your frame."

Maggie felt her blood pressure rise as she stared at Hank in the mirror. Here was this trim, firm, glorious hulk of a man, with biceps bursting out of a black T-shirt and taut, compact thighs and calves revealed below his sexy black nylon running shorts. He was whole, content, filled with an undaunted spirit. Staring at him, Maggie felt an overwhelming flood of rage and anguish. It wasn't fair, dammit. He had no right to feel so sure of himself, so sure of what he wanted, so adept at getting it, anymore than it seemed fair to her that he could manipulate her emotions with such ease. Even now, she found herself both hating him and wanting him in the same breath.

In a low, hostile voice, she said, "You can just forget about playing 'save-the-poor-waif' with me. You don't have to fatten me up. Despite your misconceptions, I'm not in need of your rescue efforts. I've looked after myself for years now, and I'm not about to hand my welfare over to you. Save it for some lost soul you'll no doubt pick up in your cab before long. Maybe then," she added acerbically, "you'll have someone new to bore with your philosophy, your theories, and your misplaced sense of humor." She stopped to catch her breath.

Hank's warm laughter completely deflated her attack. "Hey," he said, as he started doing a few leg stretches, "talk about lost souls. There was this fare I picked up at the airport this morning—"

"Oh, shut up." She moved to the corner, where a cassette player was resting on a small table. There were a few tapes beside the machine. Maggie grabbed one and snapped it in, setting the volume on high. Then she turned to him.

"You want to work out," she said sternly, her voice tinged with ruthless determination, "then let's work out."

If her dancers had thought Maggie Doyle a tough taskmaster, they would have been speechless with rage if she put them through the paces she put Hank through, especially considering this was the first dry run. Maggie knew Hank worked out with weights, but she was certain she was forcing him to connect with muscles he never knew existed. Although she did some of the exercises with him, she used her bad ankle as an excuse enough of the time to keep from doing herself any real damage. Not that she wouldn't be a little sore in the morning, but it was worth it.

She had to hand it to Hank. He went along gamely with her routine, even though she could see it was killing him. Whenever he did balk a little, she'd remind him that this was his idea.

"Besides, you're an inspiration," she said with an innocent smile. "What did you say about that boxer? He wouldn't accept defeat as long as he could still climb out of the ring? Come on, Hank. You could still make it out of this room."

Hank knew exactly what Maggie was doing, but he went along with her. Not because, as he was sure Maggie thought, he was too proud to admit defeat, but because he loved seeing her come back to life again, even if it did mean he'd be flat on his back tomorrow, every muscle in his body screaming in pain.

The forty-five minutes felt like an eternity to Hank. Maggie, fortunately, was running out of steam, and when he pointed out the time, she relented. They both fell back onto the floor mat, their breath coming in short, rapid gasps.

When Hank turned his head to look at her, Maggie was smiling. She felt his gaze and glanced over at him.

"I feel terrific," she said, her smile broadening. "Thanks." She shifted onto her side, her chest still heaving, but she was beginning to catch her breath. "How about you?"

He gave her a dirty look. "I feel like somebody just played a vicious game of handball using my body as the backboard."

Maggie's smile turned sheepish. "You better take a long, hot shower."

"Does that require moving?"

Maggie laughed, looking pleased with herself despite the twinge of guilt. She still felt that he deserved a few aches and pains for manhandling her like he had. "I guess you don't want to go rowing right now."

"How about helping me up and dragging me to my room? I'd like to die in my own bed."

Maggie stood up and stretched out her arms, a saucy smile on her lips. "Come on, babe. This time you can lean on me."

Hank took hold of her hands. The next thing Maggie knew, she was falling on top of him, his supposedly aching arms firmly wrapping around her.

"What do you think you're doing?" Maggie exclaimed. They were both damp with sweat, their faces glistening.

Hank opened his mouth and kissed her for an answer. Maggie, frightened by the surge of passion sweeping over her, struggled in his arms. His kiss was relentless, insistent, and demanding, as relentless, insistent, and demanding as her desire. Since that day in Capistrano, she had not stopped wanting him. Fighting her need constantly did not alter that reality. As her lips parted, Hank thrust his tongue against hers, his hands moving up as he began slipping the leotard off her shoulders.

Maggie finally pulled her mouth free. "We have to shower," she said in a flash of practicality. They both laughed.

"Great idea. Let's do that."

Hank rolled her over, Maggie holding her breath as he started to undress her. She grasped his hand. "Where's the shower? I think I've made enough of a display of myself today."

He held her face between his hands and kissed the tip of her nose. "Relax. I have my own private bathroom. One of the bonuses of having been the first paying tenant here."

"Good thing I got this new cast. Fieldston said nothing would happen to it if it got wet. If I had to keep taking those sponge baths, I would have gone mad." She was talking a lot, playing for time. There was almost something more intimate about showering with Hank than lying in a proper double bed making love. She wasn't sure she could handle it.

Hank leaned over her, pressing a finger to her lips. "Shut up," he said in such caressing tones that Maggie was immediately silent. Then slowly, lovingly, he tugged the green leotard down over her arms, her small firm breasts, her heaving ribcage. Maggie arched her back so he could slide the suit over her hips, his fingers gripping and pulling her white tights down as well.

The sheen of her lithe, slender body was so erotically beautiful that Hank had to fight back the burning desire to take possession of her there and then. Only the sensual image of lathering every inch of her, watching the water wash over her silky skin as he held her against him, kept him from acting on his need.

He struggled to his feet, his muscles already beginning to ache, but it didn't matter. Nothing

117

mattered except Maggie. He helped her up. She quickly undressed him, unable to resist one hungry kiss before he led her to his private bathroom.

CHAPTER SEVEN

As the cascading spray enveloped them, Hank moved his hands slowly up the curve of Maggie's hips to her breasts. She sighed deeply, her head tilting back, her eyes closed, a delightfully greedy smile on her lips.

"You're a beautiful sea nymph," he murmured, his mouth moving to hers. Maggie swept her arms around him, prolonging the kiss, feeling desire sweep through her.

When they left the shower, Hank wrapped a large bath towel around her and carried her into his bedroom. Brushing her wet hair from her eyes, Maggie looked around the room in astonishment. There were half a dozen enlarged photos of her on the wall, the largest one the shot Hank had taken of her at the fountain at Capistrano when the swallow had perched on her hand for that brief moment.

"They're marvelous," she gasped. "I look fantastic."

"How modest you are," Hank teased.

Maggie swiveled in his arms as he set her down. "You make me look beautiful," she said, then more softly added, "you make me feel beautiful."

Lifting the towel to her hair, his hands moved in long strokes, drying it off. Then he proceeded to towel her body with caressing motions, lingering over her breasts, her long slender legs.

Maggie felt dizzy with desire as Hank pushed back her hair, kissing her closed eyes, her lips, the pulsating hollow of her throat.

"I missed you. Don't ever withdraw from me like that again," he whispered, easing her down onto the bed.

"No more locked doors, I promise," she murmured, smiling as she thought of the splintered wooden frame downstairs.

Hank grinned, reading her mind. "I've never done anything like that before. You do strange and wondrous things to me, Maggie Doyle."

She took hold of the towel, rubbing it vigorously over Hank's wet hair. Then she tossed it onto the floor. In a seductive whisper, the tip of her tongue playing provocatively on his earlobe, Maggie said, "Let's do wondrous things to each other." Then she slipped her tongue down the side of his neck and over his chest to his firm, hard stomach.

A low moan broke from him, and Maggie thrilled to the sound of his pleasure even as she lost herself in the heat of pure sensuality. Her hands slid up his thighs, her vibrant red hair cascading over his stomach, driving him to a blazing pitch of desire.

Then he slid down to her, kissing her, en-

120

folding her so tightly in his arms that her breasts were crushed against his chest. His hands moved around her waist, lifting her until she sat astride him. Gently, he lifted her once more, only for a moment, lowering her upon him so that she cried out with uninhibited pleasure as she felt him slide upward, filling her, making her feel truly complete. She arched back, fingers spread wide as she pressed them hard into the mattress for support. Hank's hands cupped her breasts as their movements found a perfect rhythm. At the last moment, he reached for her face, drawing her to him, kissing her again and again until they both cried out in passionate release.

They kept touching and stroking afterward, neither wanting to lose contact now that they had finally come together again. Hank rested on his elbow, his fingers skimming her knee.

"You have a scar there." He looked closer, then bent to kiss the mark lightly.

Maggie laughed. "That tickles."

"How did you get it?"

"A nasty boy threw a rock at me when I was eleven."

Hank scowled and did a great imitation of a Damon Runyon gangster. "Tell me who it was and I'll send my boys after him."

"Don't worry. When Madame saw the damage, she went after him herself."

"You're kidding!"

Maggie grinned. "Well, she would have liked to." Looking a little wistful, she added, "So instead, she took it out on me. She made me sit out of class for three days, even though I was perfectly fine after one. That's what I got for getting in the way of that rock."

Hank drew her into his arms. "Poor baby," he crooned. "Had I been there, I would have kissed it better."

Maggie touched his cheek. "Yes, I believe you would have." Then, feeling the mood becoming more serious than she felt comfortable with, Maggie began examining Hank's body, asking, "And where are your scars? Oh, yes," she said, her eyes sparkling, "I remember. Your lip. I did bruise it unmercifully before my operation. Let me see." She ran a finger lightly, sensually over his bottom lip. "Nothing. Not even a scratch." Feigning disappointment, she said, "You must have a scar somewhere. You can't be a perfect specimen."

Hank rolled her over, pinning her down playfully. "And why not?"

"Because," Maggie retorted, "it isn't fair. Here I am, broken ankle, a glaring scar on my knee—and I won't even mention all the other flaws and imperfections—"

Hank kissed her loudly. "I love your imperfections. I love you. Stop looking like I just told you that you have a bad case of prickly heat. If it will make you feel better, I do have a few scars."

Maggie's eyes scanned his body. "Where?"

He gave her a seductive smile. "Come find them."

She never did find them, but the truth was, she

gave up looking very quickly as Hank's arms came around her.

Afterward, contented and physically spent, Maggie stretched languorously, one hand sliding idly down Hank's chest. "You know, your body is going to be in agony in the morning."

"It was worth it." He put his arm around her and pulled her to his chest.

"We better get dressed and go downstairs." A flash of dismay swept over her features as she looked into his brown eyes. "Do you think they suspect?"

Hank grinned. "I'm sure they're hoping," he teased.

Maggie swatted him lightly, then grinned. "I was hoping, too."

He smiled, his hand tenderly stroking her cheek. "So was I."

Maggie's days fell into a pleasant rhythm after that. Mornings, she worked out in Hank's spare room, Hank joining her most of the time. Some afternoons she would go to the Santa Lucia Institute with Miss May, finally giving in to the elderly woman's coaxing to run a dance class for the residents. That, coupled with her two classes a week at the boardinghouse, one for children and one for adults, brought Maggie back into the world she was most familiar with, even if she were now entering it through a new and somewhat strange door.

This afternoon, twelve youngsters, ranging in age from eight to thirteen, sat on the floor of the parlor, chattering away as they slipped into their

123

ballet slippers. They formed a vibrant rainbow with their gaily colored leotards and tights—slim, eager children filled with anticipation and excitement. They adored Maggie. At the first few classes, there had been laughs and titters as they watched the slender dance teacher wiggle about on her cast as she showed them some of the beginning ballet and modern dance positions. But they soon forgot the cast as they became mesmerized by Maggie's grace and skill. Most of all, they loved the fact that she treated them as real dancers, even though most of them had never even heard of a demi-plié or a detourné.

Maggie was firm but supportive of each of her charges, finding in each one of them something to praise, to applaud. It came easily to her, because they were so eager to please. And much to Maggie's surprise and delight, they seemed to be filled with the joy of movement, open to the thrill of letting the music envelop and carry them to new worlds. There was a purity and freeness about them, and Maggie found it easier and far more rewarding to teach them than she ever would have imagined.

Miss May watched from the doorway as the children did their floor exercises. Maggie, looking vibrant and ethereally lovely in a pale blue leotard that showed off her firm, healthy body, moved about the room guiding, instructing, encouraging.

"Now lift your arm slowly—slower still—good. Open it to the side, let your eyes follow. Very nice. Tilt your head. Perfect, Denise." Maggie patted the nine-year-old on the shoulder, leaning forward to whisper, "Bottom tucked in."

Maggie went to the next child, Kelly, a slightly overweight thirteen-year-old who was having problems with the grande plié. Maggie remembered how Madame had scolded her furiously to turn her whole leg to the side during those first months when Maggie was learning the same position. From the hip, Madame would shout, from the hip. And Maggie, struggling, would work harder, every muscle pulling, until the line from hip to toe was perfect.

As a teacher, Maggie's style was gentler, but equally demanding. "No, Kelly, don't force it. You must feel the movement, visualize it in your mind before you try to accomplish it. You're fighting against yourself."

"I can't do it, Maggie. I just can't get my body to do the right thing."

"We don't say 'can't' here, Kelly. To dance, you must use every ounce of concentration. You must be willing to struggle, to suffer, to grow frustrated—to achieve. But only with hard work and determination. I'm not here merely to pass time. I'm here to teach you to be dancers, whether you pursue it later on or not."

Kelly smiled. She, like the other children, respected and admired Maggie for her commitment, her determination not to let them slide. The young girl did another grande plié, closing her eyes first to visualize the move.

"Better. Much better." Maggie turned on the music, letting the children spend a few minutes in free expression, uncramping their muscles, stretching, turning, pretending to be prima ballerinas. As she leaned against the wall watching them, her earlier words echoed in her mind: *I'm not here merely to pass time.* It was true, Maggie reflected. She had changed. Slowly, subtly, in many ways, she had come to view her life in different terms. She knew she had many people to thank for helping her find new purpose. Miss May, Hutch, Rita, and Amy had come to treat her as part of their unique little family. And Hank—he had helped her most of all. For the first time in her life, Maggie knew what it was like to feel cherished, to feel loved. And to love, she admitted, though she'd not yet mustered the courage to say those words out loud.

She felt such a complexity of feelings; her old self was still alive inside her—returning to choreography was as sharp a desire and need as ever. Maggie was unable to reconcile the old with the new. And beneath all the confusion was the ever-present fear that her ankle would never heal properly and that the choice, no matter how much she dreaded having to make it, would be taken from her.

She looked down at her foot. In three days she would know whether the pin holding the shattered bone together had done the trick and the cast could be taken off. Even if she were truly on the mend and she could put the fear of another operation behind her, Maggie would have to accept months of restricted activity before the pin could actually be removed. It would be almost

126

like starting over. And it would also mean saying good-bye to Henry Collier August. Her career required too much absorption, too much energy, for her to juggle it with an intense personal relationship.

She was happy, maybe happier than she'd ever been in some ways, but she still saw her life at Miss May's boardinghouse as a kind of fantasy, each of its occupants—especially Hank—inhabiting a safe, loving nest, doing their good deeds, untouched by the world at large. It was Hank's generosity, his open, giving nature that Maggie found most appealing and yet had the most trouble accepting. She could not shake the notion that he was afraid to test his true abilities and talents. And it was particularly unsettling to know that he was more afraid of succeeding than failing.

They argued about it at times. Maggie had read a good deal of Hank's journal, a collection of witty, esoteric pieces on everything from evolution and the search for universal truths to the pros and cons of repairing your own automobile. Hank's inimitable personality showed on every page, and Maggie found it enormously frustrating to think that only a chosen few would ever be privileged to experience the pleasure of his writing or his exceptional photographs. But her arguments fell on deaf ears. Hank insisted that he wrote purely as a way to sort out his thoughts and feelings. And he took photographs only for the joy of capturing the moment and having the thrill of making it last on film.

"No, Cathy. You'll injure your toes that way," Maggie said, shaking her mind free of her wandering thoughts and focusing back on the children. She clapped her hands for order.

"All right, my little chickadees." She grinned. "Next class, be prepared to work your—toes off." She winked as everyone giggled. "We will do a proper pirouette on Friday, come what may. And if you're all perfect prima ballerinas, I might figure out a way to teach you some break dance moves."

Everyone cheered. They all knew Maggie had worked on several break dance movies, and they had been pestering her from the start to teach them some of the moves. Maggie wasn't quite sure how she was going to do that with her cast on, but she'd been remarkably ingenious so far in getting her desired points across. She'd find a way.

Exhausted from her workout Maggie would have loved to stretch out on her bed and rest, but it had become traditional to stay after class for Miss May's homemade chocolate-chip cookies and fresh-squeezed orange juice. By the time Maggie put away the cassettes, her young dancers were eagerly devouring the goodies. After having seconds, and in some instances thirds, the children changed out of their ballet shoes, slipped their street clothes over their leotards, and said their good-byes.

Munching on a cookie, Maggie leaned against the high-backed Victorian sofa that had been pushed out of the way for the class. Miss May walked over and gently squeezed Maggie's wrist. "Oh my dear, they're coming along so nicely."

Maggie grinned. "I know what you're thinking, Miss May. And so am I, right?"

"As Timothy says, you've blossomed into a lovely rose." Miss May gave her a teasing smile. "I do believe you've captured his heart as well as Oscar's." In a lower voice she added, "And, of course, we mustn't forget Henry's heart."

Maggie picked up the subtle hint of concern in Miss May's voice as she spoke those last words. Maggie looked over at her, wanting to say something to reassure her, but she found she couldn't. All she said was, "I don't ever want to hurt him, Miss May. We've agreed to take things one day at a time."

Miss May nodded. She was about to say something more, but the front door flew open and Amy burst into the room, breathless, which for Amy was quite a feat. She practically whirled Miss May around and actually did give Maggie a full spin. With her hair now streaked in blond and black stripes, Amy looked a bit like a zebra in flight. Taking a large gulp of Maggie's juice, she finally caught her breath.

"Guess what?" Her eyes shifted from Maggie to Miss May. "No," she exclaimed, "you'll never guess. It's just too much to believe!" She had to pause to gulp in air. "We've got a booking at The Forum. The Forum! Can you just die? We're the opening act for Jake Morris. It's our chance of a lifetime! I still can't believe it!" Amy couldn't stop moving as she spoke, her excitement radiating from her body.

"Wow," Maggie said, "Jake Morris is as big as they come. That's fantastic, Amy. I'm so happy for you."

"You deserve it," Miss May said, putting a thin arm around the young woman's waist. With a smile, she asked, "How many tickets can you get us?"

Amy grinned. "Every one of you has a seat for opening night. I'm going to take a ride over to Santa Lucia this evening and give Oscar the good news. He's got to come, too. Do you think he'll be able to handle the crowds? You know those scenes, they can get a bit wild."

"I think we'll manage," Miss May replied.

"Sure," Maggie added. "If it gets to be too much, Hank and I can take him home."

Amy kissed Maggie on the cheek. "Thanks. God, I'm so happy." She hugged them both. "Well, I'm off. Now that we're hitting the big time, it's rehearsal every day." Amy twirled around ballerina-fashion as she headed out of the parlor. Maggie and Miss May applauded. But the elder woman's astute eye picked up the glimmer of sadness mixed with Maggie's bright smile.

Hank walked into the house as Amy twirled again in the hallway. She giggled, threw her arms around his neck for a moment, then flew out the door.

He appeared at the entry to the parlor. "What was that all about?"

Maggie started to explain. But it was as though

Miss May had seen into Maggie's soul before Maggie herself had realized what she was feeling. Now, she was suddenly overcome by such a blinding wave of sadness and envy that she was unable to speak. Amy's exuberant joy flooded Maggie with the memory of her uncontainable excitement the day Dennis Arcaine had showed up with her own chance of a lifetime.

Maggie rushed from the room, leaving a puzzled Hank staring questioningly at Miss May.

A few minutes later, as Maggie stood at the window watching a young boy play with his toy boat at the edge of the canal, she heard a light rap on her door. She knew it was Hank.

"It's open."

He turned the knob and came in. "For a minute there, I thought I might have to play Superman again."

Maggie smiled. "I promised no more locked doors," she said softly as Hank moved to stand beside her at the window.

"Are you all right?"

She nodded.

He turned her around to face him, studying her closely. "I thought you just said no more locked doors, Maggie." He lightly stroked her forehead. "Talk to me."

Maggie put her arms around him, kissing him full on the mouth, holding the kiss but not deepening it. Then she rested her head on his shoulders. "It's awful," she said in a low voice. "I felt such a terrible sting of envy for a moment. I really am happy for Amy. I just—oh, Hank, one part of me feels as though my life is so full of new and wondrous things." She looked up into his eyes, a tender smile curving her lips. Then she sighed. "But there's this other part that still feels in limbo. I hate that feeling, but I can't seem to shake it."

"Look, Maggie, for a long time after I left Oregon I felt the same way. I was in limbo, too."

"But you made the choice. I didn't."

"Pretty soon, you will have to make a choice." Maggie gazed down at her cast. "Maybe."

He lifted her chin and placed a tender kiss on her lips. "I don't want you to go, no matter what."

"It isn't easy to turn away from a dream you've lived with for most of your life," Maggie argued.

"Yes, it is," Hank said, his voice a little harsh, "if a better dream comes along."

She turned her head away. "I still want that success, Hank. You can't understand that because you're so afraid of it."

Hank grabbed her shoulders, his eyes narrowing. "I am successful, dammit. More than I ever was when I was standing before cheering crowds after an election. Maggie, don't you see that success can be measured in something more substantial than fame and fortune? You have to feel it in here." He thumped his chest, his voice low but compelling.

Maggie raised her face to his. She searched for words, but finding none, slipped her hands into his, their fingers intertwining.

Three days later, Maggie sat trembling in Dr. Fieldston's waiting room. She told herself that she'd handle it whatever the news, but deep inside she knew she was fooling herself. She closed her eyes, leaning her head against the back of the upholstered chair. She could visualize Fieldston next door in his office, examining her X-rays. Was there a frown or a smile on his face? That was the part that remained blurry.

She sat alone listening to the soft strains of what was meant to be soothing music. Nothing would have helped soothe her, however. Her stomach was tied in knots, her skin was clammy, and she fought off feeling dizzy. She and Hank had argued all morning. He had wanted to be here with her, but Maggie had insisted this was something she wanted to do on her own. Whatever happened, she felt she might need some time to herself to sort out her feelings.

"Miss Doyle?"

Maggie's eyes shot open at the sound of Dr. Fieldston's voice.

He was smiling.

Maggie started to cry.

Later, when she stepped out of the medical building, Maggie felt oddly naked without her cast. She stood outside the entrance staring down at the blanched, slightly puckered skin around her ankle. Four months, Fieldston had said, before he could safely remove the pin. In the meantime, she'd have to pamper the ankle. But he didn't hedge at all when he told her she'd have full mobility once again. Maggie made him re-

133

peat it twice before his words sank in. She was going to be fine. The leprechauns had come through for her at last.

She gazed up at the sound of a beeping horn. Hutch stepped out of his Bentley and came around to open up the passenger door for her.

She grinned. "Who sent you?"

Hutch smiled. "It was a unanimous decision."

She looked cautiously into the car.

"I've come alone," he assured her. "I see it's good news." His smile broadened. "I hope you won't think me too forward, but you do have a lovely pair of ankles there," he said with a little wink.

"Not a matched pair yet." Maggie grinned. "But they will be." She did a high, sweeping kick with her now-unencumbered leg.

"Are you sure you ought to do that?" Hutch asked with alarm.

Maggie hugged him. "Let's go home, Hutch." She started to get into the car. "No, wait. Could we stop at a boutique on Santa Monica Boulevard first? Amy always talks about it. It's called Metropolis. According to her, they have the wildest, sexiest outfits in L.A. I want to buy something to knock out Hank's eyes when we go to Amy's concert tonight. And new shoes. Most definitely new shoes." Maggie laughed. "Two of them."

When she and Hutch arrived back at Miss May's nearly three hours later, laden with packages, Amy, Rita, and Miss May were all on hand, eagerly awaiting them. They cheered, hugged her, wiped at their teary eyes, and cheered some

134

more when they saw her leg and heard the good news. Maggie felt as though she were floating.

"Where's Hank?" Maggie was surprised and disappointed not to find him there waiting with the others.

An abrupt silence fell over the group. Maggie looked around sharply. "What's wrong?"

"He's upstairs," Miss May said, her voice an octave lower than usual.

Maggie started for the stairs. "He's probably still on the telephone—long distance," Miss May added.

"Oregon?"

Miss May nodded. "His ex-wife. He got a letter from her this morning, and he's been furious ever since. I don't know what it's all about, but Lucy almost never writes unless she wants something."

"I'll give him a few minutes, then." She took the large box from Hutch. "I think I'll put on this dynamite dress I bought at Metropolis for tonight and give Hank a sneak preview. The salesgirl said it was guaranteed to knock 'em dead."

In her room, Maggie studied herself in the mirror. Her dress, an extravagant and flamboyantly daring confection of amethyst colored lace and satin, was a real show-stopper. Coming to midthigh, it revealed Maggie's long legs, which thanks to her workouts and dance classes looked as good as ever. The tinted blue hose camouflaged the pasty color around her ankle and lower calf. It was almost possible for Maggie to imagine the cast had never existed. A shadow fell

135

over her features, but she quickly willed it away. After leaving Fieldston's office, she had decided to put off trying to sort things out. It was too soon. Besides, even with her ankle on the mend, there was nobody knocking on her door offering her a job.

She gave herself one final glance and headed up to Hank's room. She could make out his voice, harsh and threatening, before she got to his door. She'd heard him angry and frustrated before, but never like this.

"I warn you, Lucy. You won't get away with this maneuver. I know what you're trying to do. Don't think I haven't been waiting for it."

Maggie hesitated at the door. After a moment she heard his voice again.

"I'm catching the first plane out of here tonight. If you don't have their bags packed, I'll do it myself. You've been angling toward this move for a long time. I'm sick and tired of the hassles you give me whenever the kids get ready to come here. And this time you've pushed it too damn far, Lucy. Don't give me that crap that they'd rather go to Aspen than come here for their school vacation. Let them tell me that themselves. Go ahead. Put either of them on the phone. Lucy? Lucy? Damn!"

Maggie heard the phone slam in the cradle. She knocked softly on the door. Getting no response, she knocked louder.

Hank swung the door open. As soon as he saw her, the hard, angry expression on his face melted. He gave her a low wolf-whistle and

136

swept her in his arms. Looking over his shoulder, she saw the open suitcase on his bed.

"I guess you won't be going to the concert tonight," she said when he let go of her. "I heard the last few lines of your conversation as I was walking down the hall."

He kissed her tenderly. "I'm sorry. I'll be back tomorrow. With my kids. I'm dying to have you meet them finally." He paused, a sheepish smile on his face. "I called Fieldston this morning. I was so nervous, I couldn't wait until you came home to tell me the score. I'm truly happy for you, Maggie."

"I know you are."

Maggie made the plane reservation for him while he packed. They walked downstairs together. Hutch was sipping tea in the dining room. Hank asked him if he could drive him to the airport.

"You can never trust a cabbie to get you there on time," Hank teased, giving Maggie a pinch on her bottom. Hutch laughed and went out to start up the Bentley. Hank and Maggie lingered for a few moments on the porch.

"I'm sorry about tonight," he said. "You look good enough to feast on. Wear that again tomorrow night, and I'll take you out for a celebration you will never forget."

"I can just imagine your notion of a celebration." She grinned.

Hank kissed her, then walked down the front path. He waved as he got into the Bentley and Hutch drove away. Maggie waved back, her hand freezing in midair as she saw a taxi pull up in front of Miss May's. A man opened the door, waving. For a fleeting moment Maggie thought she was hallucinating. But the man walking up the path was very real.

CHAPTER EIGHT

Dennis Arcaine was a small, balding man in his early fifties who managed, despite his rather unprepossessing appearance, to generate a forceful presence. It was his eyes, Maggie thought. They were a rich, vivid blue and surprisingly large for such a narrow face. His nose, too, had a definite prominence, and coupled with the slight hollow of his cheeks, it gave Arcaine a strong hawklike image. He was chomping a cheroot; billows of smoke trailed behind him as he strode toward her.

Maggie had to consciously force her mouth shut as Dennis Arcaine walked up the porch steps. He seemed as surprised by her presence as she was by his. Which only added to Maggie's bafflement.

"Well, you're a sight for sore eyes," he said with a grin.

"I am?" Maggie looked clearly disbelieving.

Arcaine dropped the cigar onto the porch, snubbing it out with his heel. Maggie's eyes followed the action. Arcaine, seeing her slight frown, bent and picked up the butt. He looked around for a convenient place to dump it, and Maggie took it from him.

"Do you know that I was about to hire a private eye? This was my last lead," Arcaine said, glancing over her shoulder at the pistachio colored house. "You live here?"

Maggie nodded. "Come on inside."

As Maggie led the way, Arcaine kept talking. "Everyone I contacted at Paradyne said that, as far as they could tell, you'd disappeared off the face of the earth. A few didn't even know you weren't in New York working on my show. Castle had no leads except your old address. I spoke to the gal who sublet from you, and she gave me Hank August's name."

Maggie held the door for him and led him into the parlor. She was relieved to find the room empty.

"Then I remembered," Arcaine continued, "that August was the guy who called to tell me about your busted leg. Hey, I see the cast is off. Terrific. It's about time something started going right for me these days. I almost thought I was hallucinating when I saw you waving to me outside there."

"That makes two of us," Maggie laughed. "And just to keep the record straight, I was waving good-bye to my friend, Hank August. You're the last person in the world I would ever have imagined showing up here."

"Yeah, well—how about a drink, Miss Doyle? I've had one hell of a day. What am I saying, day?

140

Month is more like it. No, make that two months."

Maggie stood staring at Dennis Arcaine. She was still trying to comprehend his appearance at Miss May's, much less follow his words.

"The drink?" he repeated.

"Oh, a drink," she answered inanely, trying to pull herself together. "Will a sherry do?"

"Sherry?" Dennis Arcaine arched a brow.

"I don't think there's anything else, unless Miss May has something stronger put away. I could ask her."

"It's all right. I'll take the sherry. Who's Miss May?"

"She's the woman who owns and runs this boardinghouse," Maggie explained, walking over to a corner cabinet to retrieve a wineglass and the rarely used bottle of sherry that Miss May kept on hand for special occasions.

"Are you all teetotalers or reformed alcoholics?" Arcaine looked a bit worried. All he needed was to discover that Maggie Doyle had a secret drinking problem.

Maggie grinned. "Neither. It's just not a big thing here. Occasionally someone brings a nice bottle of wine to dinner. And I imagine all the boarders have a cocktail now and then when they go out."

She poured out a sherry and handed it to him. Arcaine downed it in two gulps. Without waiting to be asked, Maggie poured him another glass. He nodded.

"Sit down, Miss Doyle. You make me nervous standing there."

Maggie sat down abruptly on the edge of the sofa, dropping the cigar stub into an empty candy dish. For the first time, she realized that part of why Arcaine kept eyeing her so intently had to do with the way she was dressed. She'd been so shocked by his sudden appearance, she'd completely forgotten she was still wearing the fanciful, sensual little number from Metropolis.

"I don't usually walk around dressed like this," she started to explain.

"You should. You look great." Arcaine grinned, reaching for another cheroot. "Do you mind?"

"I don't," Maggie said, "but I'm afraid Miss May would."

"This Miss May sounds like a real winner," he said dryly. "How did you end up here, anyway?"

He might be a famous producer, able to make or break careers with a single word, but Maggie wasn't about to let him put Miss May down.

"Miss May happens to be one of the most wonderful people you're ever likely to meet. And I'm here because she was kind enough to take in a physical wreck of a woman who was out of work and feeling utterly miserable."

"Boy, was that bad timing."

Maggie gave him a puzzled look.

"Busting your leg like that just before we went into rehearsals. Jeez, did you screw things up for me."

"I didn't do myself any great favors, either," she reminded him.

Arcaine smiled. "Yeah, I see what you mean. Anyway, maybe we can still make things work out right for both of us."

"I don't follow you," Maggie said slowly, her heart beginning to beat faster. "How can we do that?"

"Chet Castle is out of the show."

"Why?" Maggie couldn't believe they'd fire someone of Castle's caliber, even if he hadn't been their first choice. In fact, Maggie had been secretly panicked when Arcaine offered her the job instead of Castle, fearing that the producer might end up regretting he hadn't gone with the number-one man. Not that she hadn't planned to do everything in her power to keep him from having any regrets.

"He was having problems with his back off and on for the first couple of weeks, which slowed us up and started getting my 'angels' nervous. Me, too, but I was trying to stay optimistic. My optimism took a dive when he ended up flat on his back for a week just when he was starting on the individual routines. It's been downhill for all of us ever since. He wanted a few weeks off to take care of the problem, but we've lost enough time. And time is money. Real pity. Castle was one of the best."

Maggie got goosebumps. It was as though Arcaine were giving a eulogy. It pointed out sharply to her how fickle show business really was.

"Chet Castle *is* one of the best," Maggie found

143

herself saying in his defense. "He taught me a great deal."

Arcaine nodded, more businesslike now as he checked his watch. "So here's your chance to pick up where we left off. We want you to step into Castle's dancing shoes. What do you say?"

Maggie's eyes fell to her injured ankle. It was obvious that Dennis Arcaine, seeing the cast gone, had assumed her ankle was completely healed. If she told him about the steel pin and about having to take it easy, she was certain Arcaine would pick himself up and walk out the door. And that would be it. How often does a second chance of a lifetime come along? As for a third—even a forest full of leprechauns, each holding a four-leaf clover, wasn't likely to pull that off.

She needed a little time. Her head was spinning. Her first impulse was to literally leap at the chance. Her second was to talk it over with Hank, who was due back tomorrow. As for her ankle, Maggie pushed aside Fieldston's warning about putting it under undue stress. After all, she'd managed to teach three dance classes a week with a cast on, including a whole hour devoted to break dancing the other day. If she decided to take Arcaine's offer, she would figure out a way to choreograph the show without causing herself further injury.

"When do you need an answer?" she asked hesitantly.

"Yesterday." Arcaine gave her a wry smile. "But I'll be in town until tomorrow night."

Maggie gave him a relieved smile. "Great. You'll have my answer before you leave."

Arcaine's eyes studied her shrewdly. "I have to tell you, Miss Doyle, I was expecting you to spill another soda over yourself in your excitement."

"I don't happen to be drinking a soda this time."

"You also seem less enthusiastic. You're not getting cold feet about handling a responsibility this big, are you?"

"Absolutely not," she assured him. "It's just— some personal complications that have developed since I saw you last."

"Can an old pro in this business give you a word of advice, Maggie?"

She was quick to pick up the sudden shift from the "Miss Doyle" to the more intimate "Maggie."

"Okay," she said, not really sure she wanted to hear it.

"The people who really make it in show business—and I'm talking actors, directors, producers, writers, and choreographers—don't get involved in fairy-tale romances. Those kinds of relationships only end up costing in terms of energy, time, and money. Save yourself the cost, Maggie. No strings, that's what you look for in a relationship. The best thing about single life is there's always another guy around the corner. There are plenty in New York. Think about it."

Maggie nodded. "Oh, I will, Mr. Arcaine. Believe me, I will."

Arcaine gave her a friendly pat on the back as

he stood up. Then he popped a cheroot into his mouth. "Don't worry. I'll light it outside."

He was still wearing a pleasant smile when she opened the front door for him, but there was a tough, no-nonsense look in his large blue eyes. "I expect to have you sitting in the seat beside me on that plane tomorrow night, Maggie. Nobody who wants to make it in this business would turn down an offer like this. You'd have to be crazy." His smile broadened. "I've seen how you work. You've got it in your blood, sweetheart. I've been around long enough to know."

Maggie was speechless. She could feel her cheeks flush. Arcaine winked and strolled down the path. He'd kept the cab waiting, but then, he could well afford it, she thought.

When she turned around in the hallway, Maggie saw Miss May standing near the parlor. She gave the elderly woman an awkward smile. "That was Dennis Arcaine," she muttered.

Miss May smiled. "Oh yes, I recognized him from his picture in *Variety*. He's a very big producer on Broadway."

"Yes," Maggie said with a small smile.

Miss May chuckled. "Well, of course you already knew that. I've made you a nice cup of tea. Why don't you change your dress and then come into the parlor and have it?"

Maggie ran her hands lightly over the lace and grinned. "Well, if nothing else, I certainly entertained Arcaine in style." She gave Miss May a quick nod. "I'll only be a minute."

She quickly changed into jeans and a striped

polo shirt and joined Miss May in the parlor. She slumped more than sat on the sofa as Miss May handed her a steaming cup of her best Assam tea.

Maggie took a careful sip. "Best drink in the house," she said with a sigh.

"Is it likely to be your last?"

Maggie shot her a look.

"Oh dear, I wasn't eavesdropping, believe me. But why would Dennis Arcaine come all the way to see you here in Venice unless he wanted you back?"

"Chet Castle's out of the show. Arcaine wants me to take over. From the not-so-subtle way he pressured me, I guess he's pretty desperate."

"And your ankle?"

"I didn't tell him anything. He assumes I'm fine now."

Miss May merely nodded, taking neat little sips of her tea.

Maggie scowled. "I didn't say yes." She paused. "I didn't say no, either. I need to talk to Hank."

"To make him understand?"

Maggie's smile was rueful. "How did you come to be so wise? I haven't been able to admit that to myself yet. But of course you're probably right."

Miss May set down her cup and patted Maggie's hand. "I'm not so wise, just old. I've been around a long time."

"I can't turn him down. If I do, I might as well sign my death certificate as a choreographer. Word gets around fast. No one in the business is going to want someone who was foolish enough to turn down an Arcaine musical."

147

"You could do yourself permanent damage," Miss May pointed out.

"My ankle? I know it's a risk. But I'll keep an Ace bandage on it and pamper it as much as possible. The cast are top pros. They'll catch on easily. I'll be all right."

"Pardon my old-fashioned sentiments, but what about your heart? Do you think you'll be all right on that account as well?"

Maggie started to answer, then realized she wasn't sure what to say. Her eyes began to water, and she sat staring off into space. Finally, in a soft voice, she said, "Arcaine says love costs too much. Hank says success costs too much, at least the kind Arcaine has in mind for me. Who do I believe?"

"Yourself."

Maggie rubbed the back of her neck. "Maybe after Hank gets back we'll be able to hash it out together."

"I hope so, my dear. We all love you very much, you know. Whatever you decide, I doubt that will change—for any of us."

It was after ten P.M. when Maggie returned home from the rock concert. She would have been back earlier, but Oscar had timidly asked her to have a soda with him when she took him to Santa Lucia. Maggie didn't have the heart to turn him down. Besides, she thought that the concert had been somewhat overwhelming for him and he needed a chance to unwind. So they'd each had a ginger ale and then, much to Oscar's de-

148

light, Maggie had asked him to play the tune he'd written for her and played that first day she'd arrived at Miss May's. As she listened to the soothing, dulcet tones on the flute, she drifted back to the evening at the hospital when Oscar and Miss May had appeared like a vision out of a dream. In some ways these last two months had been a dream for her. The question was, did she really want to wake up?

As she stood now in the dimly lit hall of the boardinghouse, she realized she had made up her mind. She had to accept Arcaine's offer. If she didn't, she would always regret it and grow to feel bitter. Maybe doing the show, being on top, would be enough success for a lifetime, and she'd be ready for love and commitment. Or maybe, when it was over, she'd realize that she'd made the right choice after all. But to stay, to turn her back on a dream that had always meant so much to her, was impossible.

The phone rang, making her jump. She walked over to the small hall table and lifted up the receiver.

"Hello?"

"Maggie. It's Hank."

She immediately broke out into a cold sweat. Now was the time to tell him, before he returned with his children in tow and the house was full of people. But her own trepidation and something in the tone of Hank's voice made her hesitate.

"Are you all right?" she asked.

"No. No, I'm not all right."

"What's wrong?" Maggie forgot about her own

149

problems for the moment in her concern for Hank. "Is it the children?"

"They're not here. Neither is Lucy. Damn it, Maggie, she must have packed them up and carted them off before I even boarded the plane. I could strangle myself for being dumb enough to tell her I was coming."

"Where did they go?"

"I'm assuming Aspen, but God only knows. It's too late to do much now. I'll snoop around in the morning and try to pick up some clues. I'm sure plenty of people know where they are, but I'm not a favorite son around here anymore. I'll tell you something, Maggie. Being back in Oregon refreshes the memory of why I left in the first place. But I still remember a few devious maneuvers from the old days. I'll find out where they are."

"And then what?"

"Then I'm going to get them and bring them home with me for the rest of their holiday."

"You mean you're not coming back tomorrow?" Maggie took a breath, trying to keep the panic out of her voice. She couldn't hold Arcaine off past tomorrow.

"I doubt it. I really am sorry, Maggie. I know I promised we'd celebrate—"

"Hank, there's something I have to talk to you about."

"How was the concert?"

"It was fine. Terrific. Soup brought down the house. But Hank, we need—"

"Hey, that's great. I wish I could have been

there." There was a small pause. "I should have expected this from Lucy. She's resented my life-style from the start. Thinks I drive a cab to humiliate her. How can she hold her head up in her social set? she asks me. Lucy never did understand me." He laughed then, a dry, rueful laugh. "God, that's the oldest line in the book, isn't it? Maybe that's because it's so often true. Maggie?"

"I'm here," she said softly, pressing her fingers against her temple. Her head had begun throbbing at the ear-shattering concert, but it was worse now.

"You're scared, aren't you?" he asked in a low voice. "About us, I mean."

"Yes—I'm scared and confused."

"Give it a little more time, Maggie. Give us a little more time." He laughed softly. "You see, I have this theory about us."

"Hank—"

"No, listen, Maggie, it's short and sweet. We love each other. We can work it out together."

Maggie ran her tongue over her dry lips. "Dennis Arcaine came to see me today."

There was silence.

"Hank, are you there?"

He didn't answer, but she knew he was listening.

"He wants me to take over the choreography for his new show. Chet Castle's back acted up one time too many. Arcaine had to let him go. I feel really bad for Chet. He's very talented."

"It's a cold, cruel world," Hank said stonily.

"He's waiting for my answer. Until tomorrow."

"You can't do it, Maggie. Even if you're so scared of what's happening between us that you want to run off, you can't avoid the fact that your ankle couldn't take that kind of strain. I talked to Fieldston myself this morning, remember? He wasn't too thrilled that you were running the dance classes at the house and over at Santa Lucia. That's nothing compared to the rigors of choreographing a Broadway show. He had to have told you the same thing."

"Dammit, Hank, don't you understand? I'm not running away. And I can take care of myself." She took a deep breath. "I took a detour for a while—a wonderful detour. Oh, Hank, I have to go to Broadway. I have to take the risk—all of the risks involved."

"I see you've made up your mind," he said coldly. "I thought you were changing, Maggie. I guess I was wrong."

"I *have* changed. You've given me so much, Hank. Everyone here—I'm going to miss you all terribly. Maybe when this show is done—"

"You'll be Arcaine's golden girl, and he'll keep you plenty busy. You'll have it made, Maggie. Number one. That's what you want, isn't it?"

"We could still see each other sometimes," she said in a hesitant voice. "No strings attached."

"What the hell does that mean? That you'll pop in to say hi, maybe jump into the sack for a couple of hours in between dance numbers, bring little gifts for—"

Maggie's temper finally overcame her sadness and guilt. "I thought you were crazy at times,

Hank, but I never thought you were downright cruel."

"I'm not being cruel. I'm being honest. That's what a no-strings relationship is all about. Personally, I wouldn't give two cents for it. No, Maggie. I want more from you. I left one kind of empty life already. I certainly don't intend to get caught up in another one."

"I wish we didn't have to—to end it this way." There was a catch in her throat, a gnawing, empty feeling in the pit of her stomach.

Suddenly, she wasn't so sure she was making the right choice. Arcaine had said there was a man around every corner in New York, but Maggie knew she'd never meet another man like Hank. After this, she knew she would not be able to manage even the rare casual involvements she'd allowed herself in the past. She knew that from here on out she would throw herself completely into her work, and she would try her best to forget that freak accident in the taxicab and all the strange and wonderful things that happened as a result. She'd try to forget that she had fallen in love with the slightly crazy, very unique Henry Collier August.

"I have a theory about good-byes," Hank said coolly. "It's better not to drag them out. Not that it's any less painful that way, but why share the pain after all the other sharing is over? Good-bye, Maggie." He gave a hollow laugh. "I won't say break a leg."

Maggie heard the phone click, the line go

dead. Still holding the receiver to her ear, she whispered, "I love you, Hank."

Hank hated whiskey. But tonight it fit the bill. After he hung up on Maggie, he walked out of his hotel room and straight down to the bar. He was on his third shot, not really feeling it, when he sensed someone staring at him. He turned his head to the right, the motion making him slightly dizzy, and met the gaze of an attractive brunette sitting on the barstool beside him.

He stared at her. She smiled. She was tall, slender, her hair swept off her face with rhinestone combs. She wore more makeup than she needed. Or maybe, Hank thought, continuing to study her, she did need it. He realized that she was older than he'd first thought.

"Are you alone?" She had a cool, sexy voice and pretty hazel eyes.

"Alone?" He nodded slowly.

"Just passing through?" She swiveled in her seat to face him. She was wearing a blue silk dress, edged with silver, the kind of dress that criss-crossed over the chest in a deep V that, depending on the position you chose to take, could be more or less revealing. She chose to make it more.

Hank didn't look away. He just smiled. Then he reached out and patted her shoulder. "This isn't going to help you feel any better."

"What are you talking about?" Her voice took on a defensive tone.

He gave her shoulder a light squeeze. "It isn't

going to help me feel any better, either. I have this theory—"

The woman had already swiveled away. She took a last swallow of her drink. With a quick, cool glance over her shoulder, she said tightly, "Forget it, buddy. If I wanted a sermon, I would have gone to church."

Hank grinned. "Yeah. Good luck."

He watched her saunter over to a middle-aged businessman sitting alone at a table nursing a beer. He was feeling the whiskey now, but it hadn't done a thing about numbing the pain. Only the anger seemed to have receded, which just made him feel worse. Being angry cushioned some of the pain of losing Maggie Doyle.

Maggie sat in the dark at the bottom of the stairs for a good twenty minutes after Hank hung up on her. She was angry, hurt—and scared. Finally standing up, she started for her own bedroom, then stopped abruptly halfway down the hall, turned around, and walked up the stairs to Hank's room. It was unlocked. No one at Miss May's bothered to lock their doors. She flicked on the light, stepped inside, and closed the door. Slowly, she walked around the room, stopping at each of the blow-up photos of herself on the wall, a vivid montage of her life and times since she had first met Hank.

There was the shot he'd taken of her, laughing in the taxicab. Then one by the canal, with Miss May's house in the background, Maggie smiling with a touch of wistfulness. She lingered longest at the photo he'd taken of her in Capistrano. Hank had told her it was his favorite. She studied it closely. Yes, she could see why he favored it the most. In this photo, he had captured the look of love that was brimming inside of her. Seeing it so clearly now, her breath caught, memories of that exquisite afternoon in the little hotel overlooking the piazza tugging at her heart. The pain became overwhelming. Maggie turned and fled from the room.

CHAPTER NINE

"Come on, everyone, let's put a little more life into it." Maggie took the terry towel draped around her neck and wiped the perspiration from her face. Then, flinging it around her neck again, she placed her back to the group of twelve dancers. "Okay, we'll take it from the top. Positions." She gave the piano player a nod. "Step up the beat a little this time, Billy."

She ignored the groans behind her as Billy started the first bar. The dancers weren't the only ones hurting. Maggie's ankle felt like someone had stuck a steel vise around it. Each kick, bend, or twist turned the vise tighter. She knew she ought to call it quits for the day. They'd been at this particular routine the entire afternoon, but Maggie wasn't satisfied with it. She was determined to have them get it down perfectly before she let them leave.

"And five, six, seven, eight." Maggie swung around to face the dancers, watching and doing the steps with them at the same time. "Over to the left, Kerry. Lou, drop your shoulder. More.

Tony, Ben, lay back. Hold it!" Maggie's voice was growing hoarse.

She sighed, holding up a hand as a signal for Billy to stop playing. "No. Something's missing. It just isn't working this way. Look, let's try another approach."

She looked over her shoulder and motioned to Al Sawyer, her assistant, who had been sitting off to the side watching as Maggie and the group ran through the routine. He was supposed to pick out the dancers having the most difficulty and work with them individually tomorrow morning.

Al Sawyer was a strikingly handsome man with straw blond hair, fine aristocratic features, natural grace, and a lean athletic build. He had been a dancer for several years but, like Maggie, preferred creating the moves to performing them. For the past four years, he'd been an assistant choreographer. Maggie felt that he had talent but lacked the kind of drive that was necessary to make it to the top. She thought he would probably always remain an assistant and would possibly be quite content with that. Not that she held that against him. Having a lot of drive was costly. Who knew that better than she? Al was a warm, engaging guy who had a lot of heart. Maggie had grown to rely on his quiet understanding.

As Al crossed the large rehearsal studio and came over to her, she suggested that they try the routine that they had fooled around with the other morning. "Only we'll exaggerate all the lifts and give it a statue effect. You know what I mean?" Maggie asked.

Al nodded. "Let's give it a whirl."

Maggie looked over at Billy. "We'll pick it up from bar nine."

They ran through the routine three times before Maggie was satisfied. Al could feel her heartbeat racing wildly each time he lifted her, his strong fingers grasping her ribcage. When he set her down the third time, the group broke out in applause. Al grinned, then gave a flamboyant bow. Maggie, all business, merely clapped her hands once. "Okay, now it's your turn, boys and girls."

She told Al to lead the group as she watched. Leaning against the wall, she was able to take the weight completely off her injured ankle. It only helped a little, but in the nine weeks she'd been working, she had learned to tune out the pain most of the time.

Better, she thought, seeing the increased energy in the dancers' movements. It wasn't perfect, but it was a vast improvement. Once again she realized that she had to stop trying to work within Chet Castle's original choreography and redo most of the staging he'd begun.

Arcaine was not happy about it. Every time he blinked, Maggie imagined dollar signs flashing in his eyes. Having arrived so late on the scene, Maggie was constantly being pressured about time. Arcaine had wanted her to pick up where Chet had left off, using most of the routines he'd already created. But Maggie had balked. She told Arcaine straight out that unless he agreed to give her complete creative control of the choreography, she'd walk out. Maggie knew that, had she not had Arcaine well over a barrel, he would have never given her such free rein with Castle's numbers.

The truth was that a part of Maggie had wanted to quit after the first rehearsal. Although she'd only been away from the business for a couple of months, it had been long enough to forget the infighting, the inflated egos, the petty hassles, the subtle and not-so-subtle games everyone played in their efforts to come out on top.

Maggie was being paid a lot of money for choreographing this show, but Arcaine was getting every penny's worth. For the past nine weeks, she'd put in grueling hours, had barely slept, and had refused to let her dancers get away with one false step. If the show flopped, it wouldn't be for want of her trying.

"Okay, Al. You can sit out the next run-through. Keep an eye on everyone, and then we'll compare notes," Maggie said as the number ended. Having caught her breath and given her throbbing ankle a few minutes respite, she was ready to go again.

"Just a couple of changes," she told the group. Seeing their faces drop, Maggie smiled. "Last time."

The music picked up. Al made a few notes, then concentrated on Maggie. He knew about her accident, and he'd noticed from the start that she favored her left leg. But despite that, she managed to carry off most of the routines with few problems. She was talented, and he noted that she had a special ability to tune into the nuances of each dancer's style, helping them use that style to their best advantage. He had to admire Maggie Doyle, even if he found her cool, distant manner and unflagging devotion a bit hard to take at times. She gave the impression of being totally wrapped up in her career, putting everything she had into it. But he sensed that beneath the fierce, determined facade was a woman who was hurting. And he wasn't only thinking of her bum ankle.

The dancers sighed with relief when Maggie announced they could go home. They filed out of the rehearsal room, their moans filtering back as Maggie called out an early call for the morning. Billy packed up his sheet music as Maggie sank into a chair, too exhausted and in too much pain to get ready to leave yet. Billy blew her a kiss, and she managed to return one half-heartedly as he followed the dancers out. Only Al remained.

"Do you want to compare notes now?" he asked.

"No. I can't think straight at this moment," Maggie said wearily.

He walked over, squatting down easily beside her. "How's the leg?"

She looked over at him sharply, not answering.

He smiled wryly. "Sorry, I forgot that was a taboo subject."

"It's fine," she replied, giving in an inch. "Just a little stiff."

"How about a rubdown?" He lifted her leg,

161

only to feel her go rigid. He set it back down carefully.

"I said I was fine. I don't need a rubdown," she said angrily.

Al gave her a puzzled look. "What gives with you, Maggie? I'm not your enemy. We're supposed to be on the same team. Aren't you satisfied with my work?"

She shut her eyes, then opened them slowly, taking in a deep breath. "I'm sorry, Al. You're doing a great job. And you put up with a lot of crap. I know I'm hot tempered, demanding—infuriating. You're not the problem. It's me."

"You? You're phenomenal, Maggie. I've learned more about choreography these past nine weeks than I have in the past four years. You've created some marvelous new numbers. They're going to be real show-stoppers. This show is going to make you."

"Make me what?" she asked ruefully. Then, seeing the shock of surprise on Al's face, she added, "Don't pay any attention to me after a fourteen-hour day. I start saying crazy things."

And I start thinking crazy thoughts, she said silently, like what it would be like to stretch out on Hank's big bed and feel his hands running down my aching leg, his lips kissing me and making me better. She shrugged off the painful image. In the nine weeks they'd been separated, they hadn't communicated once with each other, and Maggie had been unable to stay in touch with any of the others in the boarding-house even though she'd promised. She'd made a

162

clean break, only she couldn't stop thinking about Hank. She couldn't stop missing him.

"How about going out for a drink?" Al asked, getting to his feet. "My place is just a few blocks from here—if you want to stretch out and get comfortable."

"Wasn't that your wife I saw the other day, holding a baby and waiting outside the theater for you?" Maggie gave Al a cool, disapproving stare.

Al laughed. "And today she's at home waiting for me. She never minds if I bring home a friend to have a drink with us."

Maggie felt foolish. "I'm sorry. I jumped too fast into that one."

"That's okay. You're a very striking-looking woman, Maggie. I wouldn't blame a guy, married or otherwise, for trying to make a pass. I'm not immune myself, but I happen to be madly in love with my wife and I adore my daughter."

Maggie smiled, a wistful look in her eyes. "That's nice, for all of you." She got up, flinching as she put her full weight down on her left foot. "I'll take a raincheck on that drink, if I can. My ankle is killing me," she admitted. "I'm going to go back to the hotel and pamper myself with a nice, long bubble bath."

"My brother-in-law is an orthopedist," Al said hesitantly.

"Thanks, but I'll be okay."

Al scribbled the name on a scrap of paper and handed it to her. "Just in case you change your mind."

"You're a nice guy, Al. I really would like to get together with you and your wife. Maybe tomorrow?"

Al winked. "It's a date."

Maggie smiled, gave him an affectionate hug, and watched him walk out.

Alone in the vast rehearsal hall lined with wall mirrors, Maggie studied herself as she did a few simple steps. Stopping, she moved closer to one of the mirrors, examining herself more intensely. Her hands glided over her ribcage and down her stomach. She'd lost weight again. Lack of sleep, long hours of strenuous work, no time for a decent meal—and loneliness—all contributed to that. She untied the ribbon around her hair, letting it fall down over her shoulders, noticing that even her cheeks had hollowed.

She sat down on the floor, gingerly touching her ankle. It was sore, but then it was always tender these days. Dr. Fieldston would have a fit if he saw her now. So would Hank.

Or would he? She stared into the mirror. Did Hank still care? Did he ache for her as much as she ached for him? She drew her arms around her knees, hugging herself tightly, wondering when that ache would stop. She swiveled around, staring across the floor, imagining the dancers there once more.

The show was going well. In her need to fight off her pain and emptiness, Maggie had thrown herself completely into the work, and the result was impressive. Ned Weil, the director, was beside himself with excitement. He was Maggie's staunch supporter every time Arcaine came down on her for costing the backers more money. Weil kept telling her that she was a shoo-in for a Tony nomination, and she had every chance of walking off with the big prize.

Maggie thought he might be right, but she wasn't sitting up nights practicing an acceptance speech. Not that she didn't still want the recognition, even the acclaim. But as much as she tried to push her feelings for Hank into the background, they kept sneaking up to center stage and taking the glimmer out of the shining gold trophy she imagined grasping with her hand.

It was after seven P.M. when she left the rehearsal hall with every intention of going straight home for that hot soak. But a few blocks away, she passed a kiosk and one of the posters immediately caught her eye. She stopped abruptly for a closer look. Soup was in town. Maggie grinned as she studied the photo: Amy was in the foreground, dressed in one of her typically wild outfits—this one a plaid miniskirt with striped tights, a low-slung metal belt, and a skimpy camisole top that didn't reach her waist. Although the photo was black and white, Maggie could tell from the shading that Amy was still into the multicolor hair look.

Maggie's grin faded as a sharp pang of homesickness shot through her. As visions of her days at Miss May's came flooding back, tears welled in her eyes. She checked the dates of Soup's concerts. Tonight was the final show.

Twenty minutes later, Maggie was arguing

165

with a scraggly looking fellow in dirty white jeans, a glow-in-the-dark T-shirt, and a thick cockney accent, backstage at the Antheum.

"Look," Maggie insisted, "I'm a friend of hers. I know she'd want to see me. Could you just tell her—"

"I told you, she's rehearsing. Why don't you spring for a ticket and see the show? You can wave to her from your seat."

"I have to talk to her," Maggie shot back, standing her ground.

"All right, look. You hang around if you like, and when she's finished I'll mention you're here."

He walked away, disappearing into one of the rooms. Maggie found a folding wooden seat and sat down, determined to wait. She could faintly make out the music. When it finally stopped, she waited a few more minutes. Just when she was about to give up hope, Amy popped out of a door and came running toward her.

They hugged warmly; Amy grabbed Maggie's hand and led her into one of the dressing rooms.

"This is great," Amy said, giving Maggie another squeeze. "I was thinking of looking you up myself, but I thought you were probably too busy."

"I'd never be too busy to see you," Maggie assured her.

Amy swung a leg over a chair, straddling it. "Sit down. Tell me how it's going."

"First you tell me. Last I saw, you were the

opening act for Morris. A great lead-in, I might add, but look at you now."

"This is the first leg of a seven-week tour. I still pinch myself to make sure I'm not dreaming." She leaned forward toward Maggie, who was sitting on the small sofa. "And the best news of all: I'm getting married."

"Married?"

"To Ken." She giggled as Maggie's expression remained blank. "The lead guitarist, Ken Emory."

Maggie grinned. "Oh, the sexy one in the glittering lamé that the girls in the audience were falling over that night I saw you perform in L.A."

Amy laughed. "They're always falling over Ken. That's why I figured I better get him off the market, fast."

"That's really wonderful, Amy. I'm so happy for you."

"It's going to work for us, Maggie. A lot of couples split up in this business because of too much ego. But Ken and I have vowed never to set our careers above our marriage. Let's face it, this industry is strictly for the young. I can only get away with this kind of image for so long." She grinned. "When I grow old and gray, I have no desire to climb into bed with my microphone. No siree, I want a nice warm body, even if it's slightly wrinkled by then."

Maggie nodded, a deep ache filling her lungs. Amy's words had made their impact.

"How is Hank?" Maggie asked. Then quickly she added, "And the others?"

167

Amy tilted her chin. "I guess you don't know about the court hearing."

"No. What court hearing?"

Amy sighed. "It's so unfair. I could just tear Lucy's dyed-blond hair out, strand by strand."

"What did she do?"

"She's suing for complete custody of the children, that's what she's doing."

Maggie gave Amy a puzzled look. "How can she? What grounds—"

"Remember when Hank went to get the kids in Oregon?"

How could Maggie forget? She nodded.

"Well, he finally found them at a resort hotel in Aspen. I guess there was a big scene. Hank lost his temper and broke a few priceless ashtrays or something," Amy said sarcastically. "For God's sake, he didn't so much as touch Lucy's precious skin, but she called the police and made it into a major deal. Now she claims Hank is unstable and unfit to have even partial custody of the kids. The poor guy is a wreck. The case comes before the court in Portland on Monday. I really feel bad that I won't be there to give him some moral support. Miss May, Rita, and Hutch insisted on going to Oregon with him. They're going to appear as character witnesses." Amy hesitated, then looked directly into Maggie's stunned green eyes. "Look, it's none of my business, but even before this thing with his kids, Hank was in bad shape. I can't believe the change in him. He was always so happy, so carefree. After you left—"

She paused. "Hey, we all have to do our own thing. Sorry. Forget I said anything."

Maggie stood up, bent to give Amy a gentle kiss on the cheek, and gave her a wan smile. "I can't forget any of it," she said softly and walked out the door.

Arcaine was fit to be tied. It was three weeks before they hit Philadelphia, and Maggie Doyle wanted a few days off to go take care of some goddamn personal business in Portland, Oregon. He wouldn't hear of it.

"We're not even on schedule now," he argued. "Come on, Maggie. Once the show opens, you can take care of all the personal affairs you want to."

"It will be too late then. I'm sorry, Dennis. I know it's lousy timing, but I deserve a favor. I've worked my butt off for this show. Al can handle things for a couple of days."

"I just can't go along with it. Not now. We're just too close—"

"I'm going, Dennis. There's someone in L.A. who's about to go through hell, someone I happen to care about a great deal. So if you want to fire me, now's the time."

"Fire you? Who's talking about firing you? I'm just trying to talk reason. If it's that crucial—so, all right, go. But two days, that's it. Or else I might not be such a pushover."

Some pushover, Maggie thought.

Maggie spotted the Bentley in the parking lot of the courthouse as she pulled in. She checked her watch, frustrated to see that she was nearly a half-hour late, thanks to a delay at Kennedy Airport.

She'd called Miss May the night before to find out the exact time and place of the hearing. The elderly woman had been delighted to hear from her, and even more delighted to learn that Maggie wanted to come out for the hearing. She gave her all the details, as well as Hank's lawyer's name and phone number if Maggie wanted to be another character witness.

"I better talk with Hank about that first. He might prefer I didn't."

"He's left for Portland already. I didn't bother to ask where he'd be staying tonight since we're all meeting at eleven tomorrow morning at the courthouse," Miss May explained.

"That's okay. I'll just be there. I feel responsible for what happened that day in Aspen. I shouldn't have told Hank then that I was leaving. I should have just gone and explained later in a letter."

"I won't say that his mood wasn't worse because of your actions, Maggie. But I also think Hank might have blown up anyway. He's very close to those children. They mean the world to him. That Lucy could just cart them off like that —well, if I were Hank, I'd have thrown a few objects myself."

"I suppose you're right." Maggie paused. "And I suppose I'm not being completely honest. I'm not coming for the hearing only out of guilt. I'm coming because—because I've given Hank so little and he's given me so much. I just want him to know I—care."

"I'm glad," Miss May said softly. "It will be lovely to see you again, Maggie. We all miss you. Poor Rita is still trying to find someone to teach your dance classes, but no one measures up. You made quite an impact on this little neighborhood during your stay."

Maggie smiled. "It made quite an impact on me as well."

When Maggie parked her rented car near the courthouse and hurried past the Bentley, the intensity of the impact of seeing it hit her sharply. She stopped for a moment, gave the gleaming old automobile a tender pat, then took a deep breath and rushed up the courthouse steps.

A sophisticated blond woman in a tailored suit was on the witness stand when Maggie hurried into the courtroom and took a seat in the back row. From the testimony she was giving, Maggie had no doubt that the woman was Lucy August.

"I ask you, is it rational for a man who's about to win his seat in the state senate for the second time—a landslide victory, I might add—to suddenly, with absolutely no provocation, withdraw from the election, leave his wife and his two small children and go to live in a broken-down rooming house in a derelict section of Los Angeles and become a cab driver?" Lucy August managed her statement without stopping for a single breath. Taking one now, she added, "And then to go berserk because his children chose to spend their brief vacation in a luxurious resort in Aspen, Colorado, rather than share a shabby little room in that boardinghouse and go for rides in their father's taxi? I hate to say this, but I believe my ex-husband is in serious need of psychiatric help."

Maggie felt her whole body tense at Lucy August's tirade. She looked down front at Hank. His back was to her, but he seemed quite tense himself. Maggie wouldn't have blamed him for exploding on the spot at Lucy's unfounded suppositions, but she was glad he didn't. Blowing up now would only add fodder to Lucy's accusations.

When Miss May took the stand in Hank's defense, there was a hushed silence. There was something so stately and elegant about the old woman's manner that even Lucy August's lawyer showed deference in his questioning.

When Miss May spoke, her voice was firm, calm, and emphatic. She had brought photos of her house and handed them to the judge.

"As you can see, your honor, while my home might be festive, it is certainly not rundown, any more than the neighborhood. Venice is very much in vogue these days. I think that Mrs. August, for all her fine trips to Aspen, would find the price of homes quite steep on my street. Henry August has a pleasant suite of rooms with a private bath on the third floor. Both his room and the children's look out over the canal. It's quite a lovely view, as I think you can tell from the photos. And we are working on an additional

172

room on the third floor so that the children will each have their own bedroom in the future."

Miss May continued, telling the court how Hank always took a great deal of time off from work when the children were visiting, and from all she could see the three of them had a wonderful time. She spoke about Hank's generosity, his gentleness, and his strong sense of right and wrong. From the intensity in her voice, it was clear that she thought Hank was one of the finest people she knew.

When Hutch and Rita took the stand, they were just as earnest and forthright in their praise of Hank. Both of them had spent a lot of time with Hank's children when they visited and expressed their view that no one could ask for a more wonderful father.

Maggie smiled. She would have loved to stand up there and echo his praises. Everyone who knew Hank had been touched deeply by him, had been that much better for their involvement with him. But instead of speaking out, she was forced to sit silently and watch.

There was some kind of ruckus in the hallway as Rita was stepping down from the stand. All heads turned, including Hank's. That was when he saw Maggie sitting in the back and their eyes met. Maggie's lips curved in a tentative smile. When Hank smiled back, his smile was more tender and generous than Maggie felt she deserved.

The case might have gone either way, considering that Lucy August had some political bigshots and the manager of the Aspen resort in her corner. But it was the children that saved the day, especially Hank's daughter, Joanie.

When asked whether she enjoyed her visits with her father, the girl turned and gave the judge an endearing smile. "Being with Daddy is like—well, sometimes it's like the Fourth of July, all fun and excitement and surprises. And sometimes it's like a beautiful summer's day. We tell each other stories, write poems, draw, and we talk. We *really* talk. Not like, how was your day at school kind of talk. I mean deep-down feelings. I don't tell my dad all of my secrets, but I tell him more than I would tell anyone else because he understands." Tears brimmed in her eyes. "You can't say we won't be able to see him anymore. You just can't."

The judge smiled warmly. "I think I understand a little more, myself. Thank you. I wouldn't think of altering such a special relationship."

When Joanie stepped down, she raced over to her father, who swept her into his arms. Immediately, Hank's son Michael hurried over as well, all three embracing and crying. The judge didn't even tap his gavel. In fact, he looked a little teary himself.

Maggie grabbed a tissue from her purse and dried her eyes. She left the courtroom as the judge formalized his decision. She needed a few moments to compose herself. Hutch, Rita, and Miss May all came over to her as soon as they came out and spotted her. It was a warm, tender reunion. On Miss May's prodding they kept it short, however; the elderly woman ushered Rita and Hutch away as she saw Hank walk out.

He had his two children in tow, and when he came over to Maggie he introduced her briefly to them. An angry and thoroughly defeated Lucy August stormed over and whisked them away before Maggie got a chance to say more than a few words to them.

Hank studied her thoughtfully. Maggie, feeling suddenly uneasy, smiled awkwardly. "I'm glad you won. I just wanted to be here. There wasn't anything I could do, but I—" She let the sentence die.

"I'm glad." He paused. "And sad too. I hate to see you walk out of my life again." He shrugged. "Come to think of it, this will be the first time. Last time I only got to hear you say good-bye."

Maggie's heart was racing. She didn't know what to say or do. Turn around and leave, she supposed, but she felt frozen to the spot, unable to bear breaking the fragile thread linking them.

Hank wasn't making it any easier. He continued staring at her, saying nothing, as the hall emptied.

Only after everyone was gone did he finally speak. "When does your plane leave?"

"In the morning."

"You look like you haven't slept in a week," he said softly.

Maggie smiled wistfully. "I haven't done much of anything but work and miss you for the last ten weeks."

"Are you hungry?"

175

Maggie looked up slowly, a faint glow to her cheeks. "Very" was all she said.

He put an arm around her. "Come on. Let's get out of here."

CHAPTER TEN

Al Sawyer's brother-in-law, Dr. Jules Anderson, was wearing a traditional white lab coat. He was a large man with thinning blond hair, clear blue eyes, a warm smile, and strong but gentle hands.

"Does that hurt?" he asked with a tinge of a Swedish accent.

Maggie nodded. There was no point lying now. It had taken her two months after the opening of *Dance Scene* to build up the courage to follow her assistant's advice to come here.

"My doctor in L.A. had planned to remove the pin around this time," Maggie said, slipping back into the fantasy that had carried her through these past few months, a fantasy that everything would work out all right. "He—he felt that once it was removed I should be as right as rain," she added with forced cheeriness.

Dr. Anderson patted Maggie's calf and then placed his hands calmly together in his lap as he sat on the metal stool. His eyes, still warm and friendly, regarded her with concern.

Maggie looked away. "Tell it like it is."

He smiled. "Tell me something first, Miss

Doyle. What are your plans now that your work on this show is over?"

"My plans?" Maggie looked across at the doctor, but her thoughts floated off. "I've been trying to sort that out for a long time now. The musical was such a hit that I have several offers, one for another Broadway show, a couple for movies." Her smile broadened, her mind returning to the present. "When you're hot, you're hot. And being up for a Tony makes me a very hot property this year."

"You sound a bit cynical."

"I'm tired," Maggie said. "I need a vacation."

"You still didn't answer my question," Dr. Anderson prompted her.

Maggie grinned. "You're right. Awhile back—sometimes it seems like a hundred years ago—I was teaching dance to a group of children. Everything from ballet to break dancing. It's funny how I keep thinking about those kids. And then there was this other group, at an institution for the mentally retarded. I taught a class there too." She looked at Dr. Anderson searchingly, and then she said in a low, wistful voice, "I think those were the only times I was able to put my ambition, my own selfish needs, aside. It felt— good. Very good." Tears formed in her eyes. "I was happy. I used to think the only happiness was in getting what you want. Being a success was what I wanted. Someone once told me that success corrupts. I know now he meant that if all you want out of life is to gratify your own needs, care only about winning—well, then you've already lost quite a lot."

She pressed her palms together. "I need some kind of balance in my life. I want to feel good again, not just successful. Or maybe I'm beginning to see success in different terms." She paused, then met Dr. Anderson's gaze directly. "I'm not going to take any of those hot offers. Actually, I've been thinking seriously about opening a dance school for children. Partly because I do love teaching them, but there's another part as well. It would serve as a financial base for me to begin a nonprofit organization to bring dance into institutions like the one I worked at in L.A. For some of those people, it was their first opportunity to feel the special kind of emotional freedom that dance movement can give. Not to mention having fun, pure, carefree fun. It was a wonderful sight. I've talked about it with your brother-in-law. He and his wife got really excited about the idea. They even mentioned joining forces with me."

Dr. Anderson smiled. "I know. They've spoken with me about it too. I wasn't sure just how serious you were about such a project, but I can see now that it is something you really care about." He hesitated, then asked, "Will you go back to L.A. to set up your program?"

Maggie studied him shrewdly. "Al's been talking to you about more than the program."

The doctor gave her a tender smile. "Yes. You're right."

Maggie sighed, her thoughts drifting back to

179

the night, several months ago, when she and Hank had spent a passionate yet bittersweet few hours in Portland, Oregon. The next morning both of them had had to face the fact that nothing had changed. Maggie was still caught up in the show, becoming defensively angry when Hank confronted her about her ankle. She told him she was fine, he told her she was self-destructive and stubborn.

They'd finally stopped arguing, neither of them wanting to part filled only with anger. But they had managed a fragile truce at best. They said a painful good-bye at the airport, Hank returning to L.A., Maggie to New York, neither of them certain they would ever see each other again.

On the night after Maggie returned from Oregon, she was having dinner with Al Sawyer and his wife, Rita. It had grown into a regular once-a-week thing. Maggie had become very fond of the Sawyers. In a world where everyone seemed only interested in number one, Al and Rita were decidedly out of place. They were open, generous, unaffected. Rita was a dancer who had given up her career temporarily to care for their new baby. Al was equally involved with little Jessie.

Maggie was unusually silent during dinner that night. When Al finally asked her what was wrong, Maggie realized how badly she needed to talk to someone. Without giving herself a chance to hide behind her usual shield, she allowed the floodgates to open. She spent hours talking about Hank, about Miss May's boardinghouse, about

180

Oscar and the Santa Lucia Institute. When the night was over, Maggie had no clearer sense of where she would go from there, but she felt considerably better for having talked about the jumble of feelings swirling around in her head.

Since then, she'd forced herself to examine her motives and feelings more closely. Now, as she sat in Dr. Anderson's office, she was at least clear on her career goals. As for Hank—well, that remained far more complicated.

Dr. Anderson sat patiently waiting for Maggie to answer his question about her returning to L.A.; both of them were well aware that the real question was whether she would return to Hank August.

"I can't go back a cripple," she said finally.

The doctor started to argue, but Maggie held up her hand. "Don't you see? Hank would always be left with a doubt about my motives for coming back to him. He'd have to wonder if he was my second choice, that I'd only given up choreography because of my ankle."

"Listen, Maggie. First of all, I won't know how bad the damage is until I operate. I'll be frank with you. You subjected that ankle to great strain these past few months. We may have no alternative but to fuse the bone together at this point. It would mean that you could have anywhere from a mild to a moderately severe limp."

Maggie flinched, but she said nothing. Dr. Anderson continued. "In any event, I know from Al that there are other choreographers who have handicaps and still continue to work at their profession. If that's the reason you're thinking of turning down those job offers—"

"That's not why I'm leaving the business, but it makes my point. Hank would think the same thing. He has this theory"—she laughed ruefully —"he has a lot of theories. This particular one was that I worked so hard because of this need I had to prove to everyone, going back to my mother, that I was worthy of respect and admiration. He was right. If I showed up at his door lame, he'd immediately draw the conclusion that I had only given up choreography because I could no longer be perfect at it. He would assume that I felt I couldn't remain in the profession because I'd be afraid others would see that I wasn't as good as I had once been. Not too many months ago, he would have been drawing the right conclusion."

"And now?"

"Now I'm not out to prove anything to anyone. Maybe I've proved it enough with this show, but I'd like to think it's more than that. I want to believe I've learned to be less self-involved, more secure with my own sense of worth."

"Why not explain that to Hank?"

"I guess I'm not secure enough—to take the risk and find out that he doesn't believe me." She smiled as she saw that he was about to argue. "Another of Hank's theories was that I am a very stubborn woman. On that one, he's still right."

He squeezed her hand. "I'll do my best to make you as right as rain. Then you can go back to L.A. and put this all behind you."

"That would certainly be a lucky break." Maggie smiled, closing her eyes for a moment and picturing a field of leprechauns, all holding four-leaf clovers.

"And now for the category of best choreography, the nominees are, Michael Hunt for *A Night in Toledo*, Maggie Doyle for *Dance Scene*, and David Singleton for *Striking It Rich*. And the winner is—" Chet Castle, dressed in a classic tuxedo that completely camouflaged his back brace, smiled as he opened the envelope and pulled out the white card. He looked out into the audience. "Well, folks, I have to take a small hand for this one since I got her into this in the first place. The winner"—he had to shout into the mike now as people were already applauding loudly—"is Maggie Doyle for *Dance Scene*."

Chet waited for the applause to calm down. "As many of you know, Maggie Doyle is in the hospital recovering from surgery and is unable to be here tonight. Accepting on her behalf is the producer of *Dance Scene*, Dennis Arcaine."

In her hospital bed, Maggie smiled. Al and Rita Sawyer leaned over and hugged her warmly.

"You deserve it, kid, twice over," Al said.

Rita wiped at her tears. "You sure do."

Maggie squeezed their hands and listened to Dennis Arcaine's exalted praise.

"Maggie Doyle is what is fondly known in this business as a real trouper. Despite a serious injury, she gave her all to this show, and the results certainly speak for themselves." He gave a broad smile. "If you're out there watching, Maggie, I expect to see you at this podium next year accepting another one of these little beauties for both of us."

Al Sawyer turned to Maggie. "Don't tell me he bought those rumors in *Variety* that you were going to do his next show. Or have you changed your mind?"

"I planted those rumors myself," Maggie admitted. "But I have definitely not changed my mind—about any of it."

Rita sighed. "Maggie, you still don't know how bad your ankle will be."

"Come on, Rita. Jules had to fuse the bone together. And you saw his face when he told me."

"So," Al piped in, "Hank is supposed to think you're moving right along with your career."

"I imagine he'll spot the article in *Variety*," Maggie admitted.

"Why, Maggie?" Rita asked, exasperated. "Why let him believe nothing has changed when everything has?"

"Because, dammit, I'm not going back to him a cripple," Maggie exclaimed, then shook her head sadly. "I guess some things don't change. It's not just that I'm worried about whether Hank will believe I'm starting a very different career only because of my ankle. I—I just can't face him like this."

"For chrissake, Maggie," Al said, frustrated and angry, "he's not going to love you any less because of a minor limp."

Maggie looked away, her eyes filling with tears. "Maybe I love myself a little less because of it."

Rita put her arms around Maggie. "Give it some time." She pulled back a few inches, gripping Maggie's shoulders. "We're going to be so busy with our school and Project Dance, you just aren't going to have much time to feel sorry for yourself."

Maggie made an effort to smile. "Self-pity seems to have become a new habit of mine. You're right. As soon as I'm out of this place and involved in setting some of our plans in motion, I'll feel better."

Al and Rita nodded, but neither of them was convinced that that was true.

Hank read the article in *Variety* about Maggie considering Arcaine's new show over any of her other offers. Then he threw down the paper and went storming out of the boardinghouse. He drove around in his cab for several hours, forgetting to put his off-duty sign in the window, ignoring everyone who tried to hail him.

Why, he chastised himself, had he been foolish enough to believe that once *Dance Scene* was over Maggie would suddenly decide to chuck it all and come flying back to him? That last time they were together in Portland, he had seen that she was still caught up in making it. And now she had. Tony Award–winning choreographer. Her first big taste of success. Why wouldn't she be hungry for more?

He slammed on his brakes just before he smashed into the car in front of him, which had stopped for a red light. He buried his face in his hands, only moving after several motorists started beeping impatiently after the light turned green.

"Step, kick, and turn," Maggie called out, applauding as she watched the group of children at the Saint Paul Institute follow her commands. She walked over and hugged each of them. They giggled, a few kissing her, some shyly accepting her praise while others jumped up and down in their excitement. They wanted to keep going forever.

"Tomorrow, guys and dolls. I've got this bum foot, you see, and if I don't give it a rest, it gets mad at me and starts acting up. But I promise that tomorrow I'm going to have all my strength back, and I'm going to give you one heck of a workout. Can you take it?" she asked, her eyes sparkling.

Everyone shouted that they could.

Diane, who'd been teaching an older group next door, met Maggie in the hall.

"You look beat," Diane said, noticing that Maggie's limp was worse than usual. That always happened when she overdid it. "Didn't Jules say you ought to use your cane when you're hurting?"

"Who's hurting?" Maggie busied herself with her sheet music. "It's this damn humidity, that's all."

"I'll tell you who's hurting. You are," Diane

186

said in her no-nonsense voice. "And we both know I'm not just talking about your ankle. Now if instead of coming to Chicago, we'd started this program beside the cool Pacific—"

"It's a hundred and one in L.A.," Maggie said, cutting her off.

"I see you keep track."

When Hank read in *Variety* that David Singleton was choreographing Dennis Arcaine's new show, he was puzzled. Maybe Maggie had taken a different offer instead. But after checking further and learning that she hadn't signed for any new shows or musical films, he started getting worried. For a month now, he'd been trying to find out just where she'd gone. He knew she was good at disappearing when she wanted to remain incognito. She'd done just that at Miss May's.

When he finally managed to get a call through directly to Dennis Arcaine, the producer had had little to offer. The only lead he could give Hank was Al and Rita Sawyer. Arcaine told Hank that they were the people Maggie was closest with in New York.

All Hank could find out about the Sawyers was that they had moved out of their apartment, and there was no other New York listing for them.

Hank thought back to that first day he'd met Maggie, when she'd told him to pay attention to his sixth sense, intuition. Well, his intuition was telling him now that something was wrong, and he felt growing desperation to find Maggie.

He came up with an inventive plan that he thought just might work.

It was the first of October when Maggie passed a small bookstore on her way to the dance studio. As she glanced in the window, she stopped abruptly when she came face to face with herself, or more precisely, a photo of herself, on the cover of a book entitled *To Maggie, With Love*. The jacket picture was the one Hank had taken of her at the fountain in Capistrano.

She walked inside the bookstore, her whole body trembling. Oblivious to the other customers and the saleswoman behind the counter, Maggie let the tears run down her cheeks as she slowly turned each page. There were dozens of the photos Hank had taken of her, along with bits of his poetry and brief essays on the nature of love.

The last few pages were blank. On the bottom of the first empty sheet was the line, "The rest of these pages are reserved for future photographs of Maggie Doyle."

Maggie stepped out of the taxi and onto the sidewalk. She heard the cab pull out as she stood very still and looked around. Her heart was racing, but at the same time she felt a new sense of inner peace.

She looked up. The pistachio paint on Miss May's house seemed a bit faded, but the venerable Bentley sitting in the driveway was gleaming as brightly as ever. She smiled as she thought

188

about Hutch and Miss May. How much better she could now understand their enduring love and commitment to each other. And for the first time, she realized, the subtle tinge of envy was gone. Because Henry Collier August had shown her that feeling successful was more than winning. It was compassion, a commitment to others, a willingness to share, and to love and be loved.

She walked down to the canal for a few moments and sat on the grass. It was late afternoon. Hank's cab wasn't around, but she knew he'd be home soon. He always liked to get back a couple of hours before dinner, write in his journal, drop a letter to his children, spend some time in his darkroom.

Reaching into her bag, she pulled out the book of photographs that had finally brought her to her senses. *To Maggie, With Love.* The pages were already dog-eared. Once again she turned them slowly, a soft smile curving her lips as she gazed at each photo and read many of the words Hank had spoken to her.

She heard a car pull up to the curb. For a minute, she felt a rush of nervousness, but then she turned her head slowly. Hank was leaning against his cab, his camera slung around his neck, his eyes on her. When he lifted the camera to take her picture, Maggie smiled, remembering that first day when she had seen him outside of Paradyne Studios. So much had happened since that day, so many changes and discoveries.

They were less then twenty yards apart. Maggie placed the open book on her lap as Hank stood watching her. Neither of them moved. It was as though they both wanted to hold onto this moment, still only half-believing it was real.

Hank smiled tenderly. "I would have picked you up at the airport in my taxi."

"And kiss my Irish luck good-bye? Not a chance. I wanted to make sure I got here in one piece. It's been quite a trip."

His gaze fell to the book on her lap. Maggie looked down at it and then back at Hank.

"The L.A. *Times* gave it a glowing review," Maggie said. "I couldn't agree more." There was a twinkle in her eye. "You're a big success."

Hank took her in with a sweeping gaze. "Now that you're here," he said quietly, "now I'm a success."

Maggie stood up, holding the book against her breast. "I love you, Hank."

He took his camera, set it down beside him on the grass, and started to take a step toward her. Maggie raised her hand up; she wanted to finish her long journey on her own two feet. Slowly, she walked toward him. Then faster, running despite her small limp, until Hank swept her into his arms.

Maggie clung to him as they kissed again and again, her arms wrapped around his neck. Finally, breathless, she pressed her head against his shoulder as he continued to hold her tightly in his arms.

"Oh, Hank, I see so many things more clearly

now. I'm finally able to understand what you were trying to make me see—"

He cupped her chin in his hand so that their eyes met. Gently, he brushed her fiery red hair away from her cheek. Then a joyous smile lit his face and he said, "I have a theory about that."

Maggie flung her arms around him again and laughed and laughed, Hank joining in. And then, stepping back for a moment, he bent down to retrieve his camera and took one more photo of her. It was a moment he wanted to capture for a lifetime, a moment that marked a new beginning for the two of them.

Now you can reserve June's
Candlelights
before they're published!

♥ You'll have copies set aside for *you*
   the instant they come off press.
♥ You'll save yourself precious shopping
   time by arranging for *home delivery.*
♥ You'll feel proud and efficient about
   organizing a system that *guarantees* delivery.
♥ You'll avoid the disappointment of not
   finding *every* title you want and need.